Charlotte Mary Yonge

The Herd Boy and his Hermit

Outlook

Charlotte Mary Yonge

The Herd Boy and his Hermit

1. Auflage | ISBN: 978-3-73261-904-7

Erscheinungsort: Paderborn, Deutschland

Erscheinungsjahr: 2018

Outlook Verlag GmbH, Paderborn.

THE HERD BOY AND HIS HERMIT

By Charlotte M. Yonge

Henry, thou of holy birth,
  Thou, to whom thy Windsor gave
  Nativity and name and grave
  Heavily upon his head
  Ancestral crimes were visited.
  Meek in heart and undefiled,
  Patiently his soul resigned,
  Blessing, while he kissed the rod,
  His Redeemer and his God.
                SOUTHEY

CONTENTS _____

THE HERD BOY AND HIS HERMIT

THE HERD BOY AND HIS HERMIT

CHAPTER I. — IN THE MOSS

```
I can conduct you, lady, to a low
   But loyal cottage where you may be safe
   Till further quest.—MILTON.
```

On a moorland slope where sheep and goats were dispersed among the rocks, there lay a young lad on his back, in a stout canvas cassock over his leathern coat, and stout leathern leggings over wooden shoes. Twilight was fast coming on; only a gleam of purple light rested on the top of the eastern hills, but was gradually fading away, though the sky to the westward still preserved a little pale golden light by the help of the descending crescent moon.

'Go away, horned moon,' murmured the boy. 'I want to see my stars come out before Hob comes to call me home, and the goats are getting up already. Moon, moon, thou mayst go quicker. Thou wilt have longer time to-morrow —and be higher in the sky, as well as bigger, and thou mightst let me see my star to-night! Ah! there is one high in the sunset, pale and fair, but not mine! That's the evening star—one of the wanderers. Is it the same as comes in the morning betimes, when we do not have it at night? Like that it shines with steady light and twinkles not. I would that I knew! There! there's mine, my own star, far up, only paling while the sun glaring blazes in the sky; mine own, he that from afar drives the stars in Charles's Wain. There they come, the good old twinkling team of three, and the four of the Wain! Old Billy Goat knows them too! Up he gets, and all in his wake "Ha-ha-ha" he calls, and the Nannies answer. Ay, and the sheep are rising up too! How white they look in the moonshine! Piers—deaf as he is—waking at their music. Ba, they call the lambs! Nay, that's no call of sheep or goat! 'Tis some child crying, all astray! Ha! Hilloa, where beest thou? Tarry till I come! Move not, or thou mayst be in the bogs and mosses! Come, Watch'—to a great unwieldy collie puppy —'let us find her.'

A feeble piteous sound answered him, and following the direction of the reply, he strode along, between the rocks and thorn-bushes that guarded the slope of the hill, to a valley covered with thick moss, veiling treacherously marshy ground in which it was easy to sink.

The cry came from the further side, where a mountain stream had force enough to struggle through the swamp. There were stepping-stones across the brook, which the boy knew, and he made his way from one to the other, calling out cheerily to the little figure that he began to discern in the fading light, and who answered him with tones evidently girlish, 'O come, come, shepherd! Here I am! I am lost and lorn! They will reward thee! Oh, come fast!'

'All in good time, lassie! Haste is no good here! I must look to my footing.'

Presently he was by the side of the wanderer, and could see that it was a maiden of ten or twelve years old, who somehow, even in the darkness, had not the air of one of the few inhabitants of that wild mountain district.

'Lost art thou, maiden,' he said, as he stood beside her; 'where is thine home?'

'I am at Greystone Priory,' replied the girl. 'I went out hawking to-day with the Mother Prioress and the rest. My pony fell with me when we were riding after a heron. No one saw me or heard me, and my pony galloped home. I saw none of them, and I have been wandering miles and miles! Oh take me back, good lad; the Mother Prioress will give thee—'

''Tis too far to take thee back to-night,' he said. 'Thou must come with me to Hob Hogward, where Doll will give thee supper and bed, and we will have thee home in the morning.'

'I never lay in a hogward's house,' she said primly.

'Belike, but there be worse spots to be harboured in. Here, I must carry thee over the burn, it gets wider below! Nay, 'tis no use trying to leap it in the dark, thou wouldst only sink in. There!'

And as he raised her in his arms, the touch of her garment was delicate, and she on her side felt that his speech, gestures and touch were not those of a rustic shepherd boy; but nothing was said till he had waded through the little narrow stream, and set her down on a fairly firm clump of grass on the other side. Then she asked, 'What art thou, lad?—Who art thou?'

'They call me Hal,' was the answer; 'but this is no time for questions. Look to thy feet, maid, or thou wilt be in a swamp-hole whence I may hardly drag thee out.'

He held her hand, for he could hardly carry her farther, since she was almost as tall as himself, and more plump; and the rest of the conversation for some little time consisted of, 'There!' 'Where?' 'Oh, I was almost down!' 'Take heed; give me thy other hand! Thou must leap this!' 'Oh! what a place! Is there much more of it?' 'Not much! Come bravely on! There's a good maid.' 'Oh, I must get my breath.' 'Don't stand still. That means sinking. Leap! Leap! That's right. No, not that way, turn to the big stair.' 'Oh—h!' 'That's my brave wench! Not far now.' 'I'm down, I'm down!' 'Up! Here, this is safe! On that white stone! Now, here's sound ground! Hark!' Wherewith he emitted a strange wild whoop, and added, 'That's Hob come out to call me!' He holloaed again. 'We shall soon be at home now. There's Mother Doll's light! Her light below, the star above,' he added to himself.

By this time it was too dark for the two young people to see more than dim shapes of one another, but the boy knew that the hand he still held was a soft and delicate one, and the girl that those which had grasped and lifted her were rough with country labours. She began to assert her dignity and say again, 'Who art thou, lad? We will guerdon thee well for aiding me. The Lord St. John is my father. And who art thou?'

'I? Oh, I am Hob Hogward's lad,' he answered in an odd off-hand tone, before whooping again his answer to the shouts of Hob, which were coming nearer.

'I am so hungry!' said the little lady, in a weak, famished tone. 'Hast aught to eat?'

'I have finished my wallet, more's the pity!' said the boy, 'but never fear! Hold out but a few steps more, and Mother Doll will give thee bite and sup and bed.'

'Alack! Is it much further! My feet! they are so sore and weary—'

'Poor maiden, let me bear thee on!'

Hal took her up again, but they went more slowly, and were glad to see a tall figure before them, and hear the cry, 'How now, Hal boy, where hast been? What hast thou there?'

'A sorely weary little lady, Daddy Hob, lost from the hawking folk from the Priory,' responded Hal, panting a little as he set his burthen down, and Hob's stronger arms received her.

Hal next asked whether the flock had come back under charge of Piers, and was answered that all were safely at home, and after 'telling the tale' Hob had set out to find him. 'Thou shouldst not stray so far,' he said.

'I heard the maid cry, and went after her,' said Hal, 'all the way to the Blackreed Moss, and the springs, and 'twas hard getting over the swamp.'

'Well indeed ye were not both swallowed in it,' said Hob; 'God be praised for bringing you through! Poor wee bairn! Thou hast come far! From whence didst say?'

'From Greystone Priory,' wearily said the girl, who had her head down on Hob's shoulder, and seemed ready to fall asleep there.

'Her horse fell with her, and they were too bent on their sport to heed her,' explained the boy, as he trudged along beside Hob and his charge, 'so she wandered on foot till by good hap I heard her moan.'

'Ay, there will be a rare coil to-night for having missed her,' said Hob; 'but I've heard tell, my Lady Prioress heeds her hawks more than her nuns! But be she who she may, we'll have her home, and Mother Doll shall see to her, for she needs it sure, poor bairn. She is asleep already.'

So she was, with her head nestled into the shepherd's neck, nor did she waken when after a tramp of more than a mile the bleatings of the folded sheep announced that they were nearly arrived, and in the low doorway there shone a light, and in the light stood a motherly form, in a white woollen hood and dark serge dress. Tired as he was, Hal ran on to her, exclaiming 'All well, Mammy Doll?'

'Ah well!' she answered, 'thank the good God! I was in fear for thee, my boy! What's that Daddy hath? A strayed lamb?'

'Nay, Mammy, but a strayed maiden! 'Twas that kept me so long. I had to bear her through the burn at Blackreed, and drag her on as best I might, and she is worn out and weary.'

'Ay,' said Hob, as he came up. 'How now, my bit lassie?' as he put her into the outstretched arms of his wife, who sat down on the settle to receive her, still not half awake.

'She is well-nigh clemmed,' said Hal. 'She has had no bite nor sup all day, since her pony fell with her out a-hawking, and all were so hot on the chase that none heeded her.'

Mother Doll's exclamations of pity were profuse. There was a kettle of broth on the peat fire, and after placing the girl in a corner of the settle, she filled three wooden bowls, two of which she placed before Hal and the shepherd, making signs to the heavy-browed Piers to wait; and getting no reply from her worn-out guest, she took her in her arms, and fed her from a wooden spoon. Though without clear waking, mouthfuls were swallowed down, till the bowl was filled again and set before Piers.

'There, that will be enough this day!' said the good dame. 'Poor bairn! 'Twas scurvy treatment. Now will we put her to bed, and in the morn we will see how to deal with her.'

Hal insisted that the little lady should have his own bed—a chaff-stuffed mattress, covered with a woollen rug, in the recess behind the projecting hearth—a strange luxury for a farm boy; and Doll yielded very unwillingly when he spoke in a tone that savoured of command. The shaggy Piers had already curled himself up in a corner and gone to sleep.

CHAPTER II. — THE SNOW-STORM

Yet stay, fair lady, rest awhile
  Beneath the cottage wall;
  See, through the hawthorns blows the cold wind,
  And drizzling rain doth fall.—OLD BALLAD.

Though Hal had gone to sleep very tired the night before, and only on a pile of hay, curled up with Watch, having yielded his own bed to the strange guest, he was awake before the sun, for it was the decline of the year, and the dawn was not early.

He was not the first awake—Hob and Piers were already busy on the outside, and Mother Doll had emerged from the box bed which made almost a separate apartment, and was raking together the peat, so as to revive the slumbering fire. The hovel, for it was hardly more, was built of rough stone and thatched with reeds, with large stones to keep the roof down in the high mountain blasts. There was only one room, earthen floored, and with no furniture save a big chest, a rude table, a settle and a few stools, besides the big kettle and a few crocks and wooden bowls. Yet whereas all was clean, it had an air of comfort and civilisation beyond any of the cabins in the neighbourhood, more especially as there was even a rude chimney-piece projecting far into the room, and in the niche behind this lay the little girl in her clothes, fast asleep.

Very young and childish she looked as she lay, her lips partly unclosed, her dark hair straying beyond her hand, and her black lashes resting on her delicate brunette cheeks, slightly flushed with sleep. Hal could not help standing for a minute gazing at her in a sort of wondering curiosity, till roused by the voice of Mother Doll.

'Go thy ways, my bairn, to wash in the burn. Here's thy comb. I must have the lassie up before the shepherd comes back, though 'tis amost a pity to wake her! There, she is stirring! Best be off with thee, my bonnie lad.'

It was spoken more in the tone of nurse to nursling than of mother to son, still less that of mistress to farm boy; but Hal obeyed, only observing, 'Take care of her.'

'Ay, my pretty, will not I,' murmured the old woman, as the child turned round on her pillow, put up a hand, rubbed her eyes, and disclosed a pair of sleepy brown orbs, gazed about, and demanded, 'What's this? Who's this?'

''Tis Hob Hogward's hut, my bonnie lamb, where you are full welcome! Here, take a sup of warm milk.'

'I mind me now,' said the girl, sitting up, and holding out her hands for the bowl. 'They all left me, and the lad brought me—a great lubber lout—'

'Nay, nay, mistress, you'll scarce say so when you see him by day—a well-grown youth as can bear himself with any.'

'Where is he?' asked the girl, gazing round; 'I want him to take me back. This place is not one for me. The Sisters will be seeking me! Oh, what a coil they must be in!'

'We will have you back, my bairn, so soon as my goodman can go with you, but now I would have you up and dressed, ay, and washed, ere he and Hal come in. Then after meat and prayer you will be ready to go.'

'To Greystone Priory,' returned the girl. 'Yea, I would have thee to know,' she added, with a little dignity that sat drolly on her bare feet and disordered hair and cap as she rose out of bed, 'that the Sisters are accountable for me. I am the Lady Anne St. John. My father is a lord in Bedfordshire, but he is gone to the wars in Burgundy, and bestowed me in a convent at York while he was abroad, but the Mother thought her house would be safer if I were away at the cell at Greystone when Queen Margaret and the Red Rose came north.'

'And is that the way they keep you safe?' asked the hostess, who meanwhile was attending to her in a way that, if the Lady Anne had known it, was like the tendance of her own nurse at home, instead of that of a rough peasant woman.

'Oh, we all like the chase, and the Mother had a new cast of hawks that she wanted to fly. There came out a heron, and she threw off the new one, and it went careering up—and up—and we all rode after, and just as the bird was about to pounce down, into a dyke went my pony, Imp, and not one of them saw! Not Bertram Selby, the Sisters, nor the groom, nor the rabble rout that had come out of Greystone; and before I could get free they were off; and the pony, Imp of Evil that he is, has not learnt to know me or my voice, and would not let me catch him, but cantered off—either after the other horses or to the Priory. I knew not where I was, and halloaed myself hoarse, but no one heard, and I went on and on, and lost my way!'

'I did hear tell that the Lady Prioress minded her hawks more than her Hours,' said Mother Doll.

'And that's sooth,' said the Lady Anne, beginning to prove herself a chatterbox. 'The merlins have better hoods than the Sisters; and as to the Hours, no one ever gets up in the night to say Nocturns or even Matins but old Sister Scholastica, and she is as strict and cross as may be.'

Here the flow of confidence was interrupted by the return of Hal, who gazed eagerly, though in a shamefaced way, at the guest as he set down a bowl of ewe milk. She was a well-grown girl of ten, slender, and bearing herself like one high bred and well trained in deportment; and her face was delicately tinted on an olive skin, with fine marked eyebrows, and dark bright eyes, and her little hunting dress of green, and the hood, set on far back, became the dark locks that curled in rings beneath.

She saw a slender lad, dark-haired and dark-eyed, ruddy and embrowned by mountain sun and air; and the bow with which he bent before her had something of the rustic lout, and there was a certain shyness over him that hindered him from addressing her.

'So, shepherd,' she said, 'when wilt thou take me back to Greystone?'

'Father will fix that,' interposed the housewife; 'meanwhile, ye had best eat your porridge. Here is Father, in good time with the cows' milk.'

The rugged broad-shouldered shepherd made his salutation duly to the young lady, and uttered the information that there was a black cloud, like snow, coming up over the fells to the south-west.

'But I must fare back to Greystone!' said the damsel. 'They will be in a mighty coil what has become of me.'

'They would be in a worse coil if they found your bones under a snow wreath.'

Hal went to the door and spied out, as if the tidings were rather pleasant to him than otherwise. The goodwife shivered, and reached out to close the shutter, and there being no glass to the windows, all the light that came in was through the chinks.

'It would serve them right for not minding me better,' said the maiden composedly. 'Nay, it is as merry here as at Greystone, with Sister Margaret picking out one's broidery, and Father Cuthbert making one pore over his crabbed parchments.'

'Oh, does this Father teach Latin?' exclaimed Hal with eager interest.

'Of course he doth! The Mother at York promised I should learn whatever became a damsel of high degree,' said the girl, drawing herself up.

'I would he would teach me!' sighed the boy.

'Better break thy fast and mind thy sheep,' said the old woman, as if she feared his getting on dangerous ground; and placing the bowl of porridge on the rough table, she added, 'Say the Benedicite, lad, and fall to.' Then, as he uttered the blessing, she asked the guest whether she preferred ewes' milk or cows' milk, a luxury no one else was allowed, all eating their porridge contentedly with a pinch of salt, Hob showing scant courtesy, the less since his guest's rank had been made known.

By the time they had finished, snowflakes—an early autumn storm—were drifting against the shutter, and a black cloud was lowering over the hills. Hob foretold a heavy fall of snow, and called on Hal to help him and Piers fold the flock more securely, sleepy Watch and his old long-haired collie mother rising at the same call. Lady Anne sprang up at the same time, insisting that she must go and help to feed the poor sheep, but she was withheld, much against her will, by Mother Dolly, though she persisted that snow was nothing to her, and it was a fine jest to be out of the reach of the Sisters, who mewed her up in a cell, like a messan dog. However, she was much amused by watching, and thinking she assisted in, Mother Dolly's preparations for ewe milk cheese-making; and by-and-by Hal came in, shaking the snow off the sheepskin he had worn over his leathern coat. Hob had sent him in, as the weather was too bad for him, and he and Anne crouched on opposite sides of the wide hearth as he dried and warmed himself, and cosseted the cat which Anne had tried to caress, but which showed a decided preference for the older friend.

'Our Baudrons at Greystone loves me better than that,' said Anne. 'She will come to me sooner than even to Sister Scholastica!'

'My Tib came with us when we came here. Ay, Tib! purr thy best!' as he held his fingers over her, and she rubbed her smooth head against him.

'Can she leap? Baudrons leaps like a horse in the tilt-yard.'

'Cannot she! There, my lady pussy, show what thou canst do to please the demoiselle,' and he held his arms forward with clasped hands, so that the grey cat might spring over them, and Lady Anne cried out with delight.

Again and again the performance was repeated, and pussy was induced to dance after a string dangled before her, to roll over and play in apparent ecstasy with a flake of wool, as if it were a mouse, and Watch joined in the game in full amity. Mother Dolly, busy with her distaff, looked on, not displeased, except when she had to guard her spindle from the kitten's pranks, but she was less happy when the children began to talk.

'You have seen a tilt-yard?'

'Yea, indeed,' he answered dreamily. 'The poor squire was hurt—I did not like it! It is gruesome.'

'Oh, no! It is a noble sport! I loved our tilt-yard at Bletso. Two knights could gallop at one another in the lists, as if they were out hunting. Oh! to hear the lances ring against the shields made one's heart leap up! Where was yours?'

Here Dolly interrupted hastily, 'Hal, lad, gang out to the shed and bring in some more sods of turf. The fire is getting low.'

'Here's a store, mother—I need not go out,' said Hal, passing to a pile in the corner. 'It is too dark for thee to see it.'

'But where was your castle?' continued the girl. 'I am sure you have lived in a castle.'

Insensibly the two children had in addressing one another changed the homely singular pronoun to the more polite, if less grammatical, second person plural. The boy laughed, nodded his head, and said, 'You are a little witch.'

'No great witchcraft to hear that you speak as we do at home in Bedfordshire, not like these northern boors, that might as well be Scots!'

'I am not from Bedfordshire,' said the lad, looking much amused at her perplexity.

'Who art thou then?' she cried peremptorily.

'I? I am Hal the shepherd boy, as I told thee before.'

'No shepherd boy are you! Come, tell me true.'

Dolly thought it time to interfere. She heard an imaginary bleat, and ordered Hal out to see what was the matter, hindering the girl by force from running after him, for the snow was coming down in larger flakes than ever. Nevertheless, when her husband was heard outside she threw a cloak over her head and hurried out to speak with him. 'That maid will make our lad betray himself ere another hour is over their heads!'

'Doth she do it wittingly?' asked the shepherd gravely.

'Nay, 'tis no guile, but each child sees that the other is of gentle blood, and women's wits be sharp and prying, and the maid will never rest till she has wormed out who he is.'

'He promised me never to say, nor doth he know.'

'Thee! Much do the hests of an old hogherd weigh against the wiles of a young maid!'

'Lord Hal is a lad of his word. Peace with thy lords and ladies, woman, thou'lt have the archers after him at once.'

'She makes no secret of being of gentle blood—a St. John of Bletso.'

'A pestilent White Rose lot! We shall have them on the scent ere many days are over our head! An unlucky chance this same snow, or I should have had the wench off to Greystone ere they could exchange a word.'

'Thou wouldst have been caught in the storm. Ill for the maid to have fallen into a drift!'

'Well for the lad if she never came out of it!' muttered the gruff old shepherd. 'Then were her tongue stilled, and those of the clacking wenches at York—Yorkists every one of them.'

Mother Dolly's eyes grew round. 'Mind thee, Hob!' she said; 'I ken thy bark is worse than thy bite, but I would have thee to know that if aught befall the maid between this and Greystone, I shall hold thee—and so will my Lady —guilty of a foul deed.'

'No fouler than was done on the stripling's father,' muttered the shepherd. 'Get thee in, wife! Who knows what folly those two may be after while thou art away? Mind thee, if the maid gets an inkling of who the boy is, it will be the worse for her.'

'Oh!' murmured the goodwife, 'I moaned once that our Piers there should be deaf and well-nigh dumb, but I thank God for it now! No fear of perilous word going out through him, or I durst not have kept my poor sister's son!'

Mother Doll trusted that her husband would never have the heart to leave the pretty dark-haired girl in the snow, but she was relieved to find Hal marking down on the wide flat hearth-stone, with a bit of charcoal, all the stars he had observed. 'Hob calls that the Plough—those seven!' he said; 'I call it Charles's Wain!'

'Methinks I have seen that!' she said, 'winter and summer both.'

'Ay, he is a meuseful husbandman, that Charles! And see here! This middle mare of the team has a little foal running beside her'—he made a small spot beside the mark that stood for the central star of what we call the Bear's Tail.

'I never saw that!'

'No, 'tis only to be seen on a clear bright night. I have seen it, but Hob mocks at it. He thinks the only use of the Wain is to find the North Star, up beyond there, pointing by the back of the Plough, and go by it when you are lost.'

'What good would finding the North Star do? It would not have helped me home if you had not found me!'

'Look here, Lady Anne! Which way does Greystone lie?'

'How should I tell?'

'Which way did the sun lie when you crossed the moor?'

Anne could not remember at first, but by-and-by recollected that it dazzled her eyes just as she was looking for the runaway pony; and Hal declared that it proved that the convent must have been to the south of the spot of her fall; but his astronomy, though eagerly demonstrated, was not likely to have brought her back to Greystone. Still Doll was thankful for the safe subject, as he went on to mark out what he promised that she should see in the winter—the swarm of glow-worms, as he called the Pleiades; and 'Our Lady's Rock,' namely, distaff, the northern name for Orion; and then he talked of the stars that so perplexed him, namely, the planets, that never stayed in their places.

By-and-by, when Mother Dolly's work was over the kettle was on the fire, and she was able to take out her own spinning, she essayed to fill up the time by telling them lengthily the old stories and ballads handed down from minstrel to minstrel, from nurse to nurse, and they sat entranced, listening to the stories, more than even Hal knew she possessed, and holding one another by the hand as they listened.

Meantime the snow had ceased—it was but a scud of early autumn on the mountains—the sun came out with bright slanting beams before his setting, there was a soft south wind; and Hob, when he came in, growled out that the thaw had set in, and he should be able to take the maid back in the morning. He sat scowling and silent during supper, and ordered Hal about with sharp sternness, sending him out to attend to the litter of the cattle, before all had finished, and manifestly treated him as the shepherd's boy, the drudge of the house, and threatening him with a staff if he lingered, soon following himself. Mother Dolly insisted on putting the little lady to bed before they should return, and convent-bred Anne had sufficient respect for proprieties to see that it was becoming. She heard no more that night.

CHAPTER III. — OVER THE MOOR

In humblest, simplest habit clad,
  But these were all to me.—GOLDSMITH.

'Hal! What is your name?'

She stood at the door of the hovel, the rising sun lighting up her bright dark eyes, and smiling in the curly rings of her hair while Hal stood by, and Watch bounded round them.

'You have heard,' he said, half smiling, and half embarrassed.

'Hal! That's no name.'

'Harry, an it like you better.'

'Harry what?' with a little stamp of her foot.

'Harry Hogward, as you see, or Shepherd, so please you.'

'You are no Hogward, nor shepherd! These folk be no kin to you, I can see. Come, an you love me, tell me true! I told you true who I am, Red Rose though I see you be! Why not trust me the same?'

'Lady, I verily ken no name save Harry. I would trust you, verily I would, but I know not myself.'

'I guess! I guess!' she cried, clapping her hands, but at the moment Dolly laid a hand on her shoulder.

'Do not guess, maiden,' she said. 'If thou wouldst not bring evil on the lad that found thee, and the roof that sheltered thee, guess not, yea, and utter not a word save that thou hast lain in a shepherd's hut. Forget all, as though thou hadst slept in the castle on the hill that fades away with the day.'

She ended hastily, for her husband was coming up with a rough pony's halter in his hand. He was in haste to be off, lest a search for the lost child might extend to his abode, and his gloomy displeasure and ill-masked uneasiness reduced every-one to silence in his presence.

'Up and away, lady wench!' he said. 'No time to lose if you are to be at Greystone ere night! Thou Hal, thou lazy lubber, go with Piers and the sheep —'

'I shall go with you,' replied Hal, in a grave tone of resolution. 'I will only go within view of the convent, but go with you I will.'

He spoke with a decided tone of authority, and Hob Hogward muttered a little to himself, but yielded.

Hal assisted the young lady to mount, and they set off along the track of the moss, driving the cows, sheep, and goats before them—not a very considerable number—till they came to another hut, much smaller and more rude than that where they had left Mother Doll.

Piers was a wild, shaggy-haired lad, with a sheepskin over his shoulders, and legs bare below the knee, and to him the charge of the flock was committed, with signs which he evidently understood and replied to with a gruff 'Ay, ay!' The three went on the way, over the slope of a hill, partly clothed with heather, holly and birch trees, as it rose above the moss. Hob led the pony, and there was something in his grim air and manner that hindered any conversation between the two young people. Only Hal from time to time gathered a flower for the young lady, scabious and globe flowers, and once a very pink wild rose, mingled with white ones. Lady Anne took them with a meaning smile, and a merry gesture, as though she were going to brush Hal's face with the petals. Hal laughed, and said, 'You will make them shed.'

'Well and good, so the disputes be shed,' said Anne, with more meaning than perhaps Hal understood. 'And the white overcomes the red.'

'May be the red will have its way with spring—'

But there Hob looked round on them, and growled out, 'Have done with that folly! What has a herd boy like thee to do with roses and frippery? Come away from the lady's rein. Thou art over-held to thrust thyself upon her.'

Nevertheless, as Hal fell back, the dark eyes shot a meaning glance at him, and the party went on in silence, except that now and then Hob launched at Hal an order that he endeavoured to render savagely contemptuous and harsh, so that Lady Anne interfered to say, 'Nay, the poor lad is doing no harm.'

'Scathe enough,' answered Hob. 'He always will be doing ill if he can. Heed him not, lady, it only makes him the more malapert.'

'Malapert,' repeated Anne, not able to resist a little teasing of the grim escort; 'that's scarce a word of the dales. 'Tis more like a man-at-arms.'

This Hob would not hear, and if he did, it produced a rough imprecation on the pony, and a sharp cut with his switch.

They had crossed another burn, travelled through the moss, and mounted to the brow of another hill, when, far away against the sky, on the top of yet another height, were to be seen moving figures, not cattle, but Anne recognised them at once. 'Men-at-arms! archers! lances! A search party for me! The Prioress must have sent to the Warden's tower.'

'Off with thee, lad!' said Hob, at once turning round upon Hal. 'I'll not have thee lingering to gape at the men-at-arms! Off I say, or—'

He raised his stout staff as though to beat the boy, who looked up in his face with a laugh, as if in very little alarm at his threat, smiled up in the young lady's face, and as she held out her hand with 'Farewell, Hal; I'll keep your rose-leaves in my breviary,' he bent over and kissed the fingers.

'How now! This impudence passes! As if thou wert of the same blood as the damsel!' exclaimed Hob in considerable anger, bringing down his stick. 'Away with thee, ill-bred lubber! Back to thy sheep, thou lazy loiterer! Get thee gone and thy whelp with thee!'

Hal obeyed, though not without a parting grin at Anne, and had sped away down the side of the hill, among the hollies and birches, which entirely concealed him and the bounding puppy.

Hob went on in a gruff tone: 'The insolence of these loutish lads! See you, lady, he is a stripling that I took up off the roadside out of mere charity, and for the love of Heaven—a mere foundling as you may say, and this is the way he presumes!'

'A foundling, sayest thou?' said Anne, unable to resist teasing him a little, and trying to gratify her own curiosity.

'Ay, you may say so! There's a whole sort of these orphans, after all the bad luck to the land, to be picked up on every wayside.'

'On Towton Moor, mayhap,' said Anne demurely, as she saw her surly guide start. But he was equal to the occasion, and answered:

'Ay, ay, Towton Moor; 'twas shame to see such bloody work; and there were motherless and fatherless children, stray lambs, to be met with, weeping their little hearts out, and starving all around unless some good Christian took pity on them.'

'Was Hal one of these?' asked Lady Anne.

'I tell you, lady, I looked into a church that was full of weeping and wailing folk, women and children in deadly fear of the cruel, bloody-minded York folk, and the Lord of March that is himself King Edward now, a murrain on him!'

'Don't let those folk hear you say so!' laughed Lady Anne. 'They would think nothing of hauling thee off for a black traitor, or hanging thee up on the first tree stout enough to bear thee.'

She said it half mischievously, but the only effect was a grunt, and a stolid shrug of his shoulders, nor did he vouchsafe another word for the rest of the way before they came through the valley, and through the low brushwood on the bank, and were in sight of the search party, who set up a joyful halloo of welcome on perceiving her.

A young man, the best mounted and armed, evidently an esquire, rode forward, exclaiming, 'Well met, fair Lady Anne! Great have been the Mother Prioress's fears for you, and she has called up half the country side, lest you should be fallen into the hands of Robin of Redesdale, or some other Lancastrian rogue.'

'Much she heeded me in comparison with hawk and heron!' responded Anne. 'Thanks for your heed, Master Bertram.'

'I must part from thee and thy sturdy pony. Thanks for the use of it,' added she, as the squire proceeded to take her from the pony. He would have lifted her down, but she only touched his hand lightly and sprang to the ground, then stood patting its neck. 'Thanks again, good pony. I am much beholden to thee, Gaffer Hob! Stay a moment.'

'Nay, lady, it would be well to mount you behind Archie. His beast is best to carry a lady.'

Archie was an elderly man, stout but active, attached to the service of the convent. He had leapt down, and was putting on a belt, and arranging a pad for the damsel, observing, 'Ill hap we lost you, damsel! I saw you not fall.'

'Ay,' returned Anne, 'your merlin charmed you far more. Master Bertram, the loan of your purse. I would reward the honest man who housed me.'

Bertram laughed and said, tossing up the little bag that hung to his girdle, 'Do you think, fair damsel, that a poor Border squire carries about largesse in gold and silver? Let your clown come with us to Greystone, and thence have what meed the Prioress may bestow on him, for a find that your poor servant would have given worlds to make.'

'Hearest thou, Hob?' said Anne. 'Come with us to the convent, and thou shalt have thy guerdon.'

Hob, however, scratched his head, with a more boorish air than he had before manifested, and muttered something about a cow that needed his attention, and that he could not spare the time from his herd for all that the Prioress was like to give him.

'Take this, then,' said Anne, disengaging a gold clasp from her neck, and giving it to him. 'Bear it to the goodwife and bid her recollect me in her prayers.'

'I shall come and redeem it from thee, sulky carle as thou art,' said

Bertram. 'Such jewels are not for greasy porridge-fed housewives. Hark thee, have it ready for me! I shall be at thy hovel ere long'—as Anne waved to Hob when she was lifted to her seat.

But Hob had already turned away, and Anne, as she held on by Archie's leathern belt, in her gay tone was beginning to defend him by declaring that porridge and grease did not go together, so the nickname was not rightly bestowed on the kindly goodwife.

'Ay! Greasy from his lord's red deer,' said Bertram, 'or his tainted mutton. Trust one of these herds, and a sheep is tainted whenever he wants a good supper. Beshrew me but that stout fellow looks lusty and hearty enough, as if he lived well.'

'They were good and kind, and treated me well,' said Anne. 'I should be dead if they had not succoured me.'

'The marvel is you are not dead with the stench of their hovel, and the foulness of their food.'

'It was very good food—milk, meat, and oaten porridge,' replied Anne.

'Marvellous, I say!' cried Bertram with a sudden thought. 'Was it not said that there were some of those traitorous Lancastrian folk lurking about the mountains and fells? That rogue had the bearing of a man-at-arms, far more than of a mere herd. Deemedst thou not so, Archie?' to the elderly man who rode before the young damsel.

'Herdsmen here are good with the quarter-staff. They know how to stand against the Scots, and do not get bowed like our Midland serfs,' put in Anne, before Archie could answer, which he did with something of a snarl, as Bertram laughed somewhat jeeringly, and declared that the Lady Anne had become soft-hearted. She looked down at her roses, but in the dismounting and mounting again the petals of the red rose had floated away, and nothing was left of it save a slender pink bud enclosed within a dark calyx.

Archie, hard pressed, declared, 'There are poor fellows lurking about here and there, but bad blood is over among us. No need to ferret about for them.'

'Eh! Not when there may be a lad among them for whose head the king and his brothers would give the weight of it in gold nobles?'

Anne shivered a little at this, but she cried out, 'Shame on you, Master Bertram Selby, if you would take a price for the head of a brave foe! You, to aspire to be a knight!'

'Nay, lady, I was but pointing out to Archie and the other grooms here, how they might fill their pouches if they would. I verily believe thou knowst of some lurking-place, thou art so prompt to argue! Did I not see another with thee, who made off when we came in view? Say! Was he a blood-stained Clifford? I heard of the mother having married in these parts.'

'He was Hob Hogward's herd boy,' answered Anne, as composedly as she could. 'He hied him back to mind his sheep.'

Nor would Anne allow another word to be extracted from her ere the grey walls of the Priory of Greystone rose before her, and the lay Sister at the gate shrieked for joy at seeing her riding behind Archie.

CHAPTER IV. — A SPORTING PRIORESS

Yet nothing stern was she in cell,
  And the nuns loved their abbess well.—SCOTT.

The days of the Wars of the Roses were evil times for the discipline of convents, which, together with the entire Western Church, suffered from the feuds of the Popes with the Italian princes.

Small remote houses, used as daughters or auxiliaries to the large convents, were especially apt to fall into a lax state, and in truth the little priory of Greystone, with its half-dozen of Sisters, had been placed under the care of the Lady Agnes Selby because she was too highly connected to be dealt with sharply, and too turbulent and unmanageable for the soberminded house at York. So there she was sent, with the deeply devout and strict Sister Scholastica, to keep the establishment in order, and deal with the younger nuns and lay Sisters. Being not entirely out of reach of a raid from the Scottish border, it was hardly a place for the timid, although the better sort of moss troopers generally spared monastic houses. Anne St. John had been sent thither at the time when Queen Margaret was making her attempt in the north, where the city of York was Lancastrian, as the Mother Abbess feared that her presence might bring vengeance upon the Sisterhood.

There was no great harm in the Mother Agnes, only she was a maiden whom nothing but family difficulties could have forced into a monastic life— a lively, high-spirited, out-of-door creature, whom the close conventionalities of castle life and even whipping could not tame, and who had been the despair of her mother and of the discreet dames to whom her first childhood had been committed, to say nothing of a Lady Abbess or two. Indeed, from the Mother of Sopwell, Dame Julian Berners, she had imbibed nothing but a vehement taste for hawk, horse, and hound. The recluses of St. Mary, York, after being heartily scandalised by her habits, were far from sorry to have a good excuse for despatching her to their outlying cell, where, as they observed, she would know how to show a good face in case the Armstrongs came over the Border.

She came flying down on the first rumour of Lady Anne's return, her veil turned back, her pace not at all accordant with the solemn gait of a Prioress, her arms outstretched, her face, not young nor handsome, but sunburnt, weather-beaten and healthy, and full of delight. 'My child, my Nan, here thou art! I was just mounting to seek for thee to the west, while Bertram sought again over the mosses where we sent yester morn. Where hast thou been in the snow?'

'A shepherd took me to his hut, Lady Mother,' answered Anne rather coldly.

'Little didst thou think of our woe and grief when thy palfrey was found standing riderless at the stable door, and Sister Scholastica told us that there he had been since nones! And she had none to send in quest but Cuddie, the neatherd.'

'My palfrey fell with me when you were in full chase of hawk and heron, 'and none ever turned a head towards me nor heard me call.'

'Poor maid! But it was such a chase as never you did watch. On and on went the heron, the falcon ever mounting higher and higher, till she was but a speck in the clouds, and Tam Falconer shouting and galloping, mad lest she should go down the wind. Methought she would have been back to Norroway, the foul jade!'

'Did you capture her, Mother?' asked Anne.

'Ay, she pounced at last, and well-nigh staked herself on the heron's beak! But we had a long ride, and were well-nigh at the Tyne before we had caught her. Full of pranks, but a noble hawk, as I shall write to my brother by the next messenger that comes our way. I call it a hawk worth her meat that leads one such a gallop.'

'What would you have done, reverend Mother, if she had crossed the Border?' asked Bertram.

'Ridden after her. No Scot would touch a Lady Prioress on the chase,' responded Mother Agnes, looking not at all like a reverend Mother. 'Now, poor Anne, thou must be hungered. Thou shalt eat with Master Bertram and me in the refectory anon. Take her, Sister Joan, and make her ready to break her fast with us.'

Anne quickly went to her chamber. It was not quite a cell, the bare stone walls being hung with faded woollen tapestry, the floor covered with a deerskin, the small window filled with dark green glass, a chest serving the double purpose of seat and wardrobe, and further, a bed hung with thick curtains, in which she slept with the lay Sister, Joan, who further fetched a wooden bowl of water from the fountain in the court that she might wash her face and hands. She changed her soiled riding-dress for a tight-fitting serge garment of dark green with long hanging sleeves, assisted by Joan, who also arranged her dark hair in two plaits, and put over it a white veil, fastened over a framework to keep it from hanging too closely.

All the time Joan talked, telling of the fright the Mother had been in when the loss of the Lady Anne had been discovered, and how it was feared that she had been seized by Scottish reivers, or lost in the snow on the hills, or captured by the Lancastrians.

'For there be many of the Red Rose rogues about on the mosses— comrades, 'tis said, of that noted thief Robin of Redesdale.'

'I was with good folk, in a shepherd's sheiling,' replied Anne.

'Ay, ay. Out on the north hill, methinks.'

'Nay. Beyond Deadman's Pool,' said Anne. 'By Blackreed Moss. That was where the pony fell.'

'Blackreed Moss! That moor belongs to the De Vescis, the blackest Lancaster fellow of all! His daughter is the widow of the red-handed Clifford, who slew young Earl Edmund on Wakefield Bridge. They say her young son is in hiding in some moss in his lands, for the King holds him in deadly feud for his brother's death.'

'He was a babe, and had nought to do with it,' said Anne.

'He is of his father's blood,' returned Sister Joan, who in her convent was still a true north country woman. 'Ay, Lady Anne, you from your shires know nought of how deep goes the blood feud in us of the Borderland! Ay, lady, was not mine own grandfather slain by the Musgrave of Leit Hill, and did not my father have his revenge on his son by Solway Firth? Yea, and now not a Graeme can meet a Musgrave but they come to blows.'

'Nay, but that is not what the good Fathers teach,' Anne interposed.

'The Fathers have neither chick nor child to take up their quarrel. They know nought about blood crying for blood! If King Edward caught that brat of Clifford he would make him know what 'tis to be born of a bloody house.'

Anne tried to say something, but the lay Sister pushed her along. 'There, there, go you down—you know nothing about what honour requires of you! You are but a south country maid, and have no notion of what is due to them one came from.'

Joan Graeme was only a lay Sister, her father a small farmer when not a moss trooper; but all the Border, on both sides, had the strongest ideas of persistent vendetta, such as happily had never been held in the midland and southern counties, where there was less infusion of Celtic blood. Anne was a good deal shocked at the doctrine propounded by the attendant Sister, a mild, good-natured woman in daily life, but the conversation confirmed her suspicions, and put her on her guard as she remembered Hob's warning. She had liked the shepherd lad far too much, and was far too grateful to him, to utter a word that might give him up to the revengers of blood.

At the foot of the stone stairs that led into the quadrangle she met the black-robed, heavily hooded Sister Scholastica on her way to the chapel. The old nun held out her arms. 'Safely returned, my child! God be thanked! Art thou come to join thy thanksgiving with ours at this hour of nones?'

'Nay, I am bound to break my fast with the Mother and Master Bertram.'

'Ah! thou must needs be hungered! It is well! But do but utter thy thanks to Him Who kept thee safe from the storm and from foul doers.'

Anne did not break away from the good Sister, but went as far as the chapel porch, was touched with holy water, and bending her knee, uttered in a low voice her 'Gratias ago,' then hastened across the court to the refectory, where the Prioress received her with a laugh and, 'So Sister Scholastica laid hands on thee; I thought I should have to come and rescue thee ere the grouse grew cold.'

Bertram, as a courteous squire of dames, came forward bowing low, and the party were soon seated at the board—literally a board, supported upon trestles, only large enough to receive the Prioress, the squire and the recovered girl, but daintily veiled in delicate white napery.

It was screened off from the rest of the refectory, where the few Sisters had already had their morning's meal after Holy Communion; and from it there was a slight barrier, on the other side of which Bertram Selby ought to have been, but rules sat very lightly on the Prioress Selby. Bertram was of kin to her, and she had no demur as to admitting him to her private table. He was, in fact, a squire of the household of the Marquess of Montagu, brother of the Kingmaker and had been despatched with letters to the south. He had made a halt at his cousin's priory, had been persuaded to join in flying the new hawks, and then had first been detained by the snow-storm, and then joined in the quest for the lost Lady Anne St. John.

No doubt had then arisen that the Nevils were firm in their attachment to Edward IV., and, as a consequence, in enmity to the House of Clifford, and both these scions of Selby had been excited at a rumour that the widow of the Baron who had slain young Edmund of York had married Sir Lancelot Threlkeld of Threlkeld, and that her eldest son, the heir of the line, might be hidden somewhere on the De Vesci estates.

Bertram had already told the Prioress that his men had spied a lad accompanying the shepherd who escorted the lady, and who, he thought, had a certain twang of south country speech; and no sooner had he carved for the ladies, according to the courtly duty of an esquire, than the inquiry began as to who had found the maiden and where she had been lodged. Prioress Agnes, who had already broken her fast, sat meantime with the favourite hawk on her wrist and a large dog beside her, feeding them alternately with the bones of the grouse.

'Come, tell us all, sweet Nan! Where wast thou in that untimely snowstorm? In a cave, starved with cold, eh?'

'I was safe in a cabin with a kind old gammer.'

'Eh! And how cam'st thou there? Wandering thither?'

'Nay, the shepherd heard me call.'

'The shepherd! What, the churl that came with thee?'

'He carried me to the hut.'

Anne was on her guard, though Bertram probed her well. Was there only one shepherd? Was there not a boy with her on the hill-side where Bertram met her? The shepherd lad in sooth! What became of him? The shepherd sent him back, he had been too long away from his flock. What was his name? What was the shepherd's name? Who was his master? Anne did not know— she had heard no names save Hob and Hal, she had seen no arms, she had heard nothing southland. The lad was a mere herd-boy, ordered out to milk ewes and tend the sheep. She answered briefly, and with a certain sullenness, and young Selby at last turned on her. 'Look thee here, fair lady, there's a saying abroad that the heir of the red-handed House of Clifford is lurking here, on the look-out to favour Queen Margaret and her son. Couldst thou put us on the scent, King Edward would favour thee and make thee a great dame, and have thee to his Court—nay, maybe give thee what is left of the barony of Clifford.'

'I know nothing of young lords,' sulkily growled Anne, who had been hitherto busy with her pets, striking her hand on the table.

'And I tell thee, Bertram Selby,' exclaimed the Prioress, 'that if thou art ware of a poor fatherless lad lurking in hiding in these parts, it is not the part of an honest man to seek him out for his destruction, and still less to try to make the maid he rescued betray him. Well done, little Anne, thou knowest how to hold thy tongue.'

'Reverend Mother,' expostulated Bertram, 'if you knew what some would give to be on the scent of the wolf-cub!'

'I know not, nor do I wish to know, for what price a Selby would sell his honour and his bowels of mercy,' said Mother Agnes. 'Come away, Nan; thou hast done well.'

Bertram muttered something about having thought her a better Yorkist, women not understanding, and mischief that might be brewing; but the Prioress, taking Anne by the hand, went her way, leaving Bertram standing confused.

'Oh, mother,' sighed Anne, 'do you think he will go after him? He will think I was treacherous!'

'I doubt me whether he will dare,' said the Prioress. 'Moreover, it is too late in the day for a search, and another snow-shower seems coming up again. I cannot turn the youth, my kinsman, from my door, and he is safer here than on his quest, but he shall see no more of thee or me to-night. I may hold that Edward of March has the right, but that does not mean hunting down an orphan child.'

'Mother, mother, you are good indeed!' cried Anne, almost weeping for joy.

Bertram, though hurt and offended, was obliged by advance of evening to remain all night in the hospitium, with only the chaplain to bear him company, and it was reported that though he rode past Blackpool, no trace of shepherd or hovel was found.

CHAPTER V. — MOTHER AND SON

My own, my own, thy fellow-guest
  I may not be, but rest thee, rest—
  The lowly shepherd's life is best.
  —WORDSWORTH.

The Lady Threlkeld stood in the lower storey of her castle, a sort of rough-built hall or crypt, with a stone stair leading upward to the real castle hall above, while this served as a place where she met her husband's retainers and the poor around, and administered to their wants with her own hands, assisted by the maidens of her household.

Among the various hungry and diseased there limped in a sturdy beggar with a wallet on his back, and a broad shady hat, as though on pilgrimage. He was evidently a stranger among the rest, and had his leg and foot bound up, leaning heavily on a stout staff.

'Italy pilgrim, what ails thee?' demanded the lady, as he approached her.

'Alack, noble dame! we poor pilgrims must ever be moving on, however much it irks foot and limb, over these northern stones,' he answered, and his accent and tone were such that a thrill seemed to pass over the lady's whole person, but she controlled it, and only said, 'Tarry till these have received their alms, then will I see to thee and thy maimed foot. Give him a stool, Alice, while he waits.'

The various patients who claimed the lady's assistance were attended to, those who needed food were relieved, and in due time the hall was cleared, excepting of the lady, an old female servant, and Hob, who had sat all the time with his foot on a stool, and his back against the wall, more than half asleep after the toils and long journey of the night.

Then the Lady Threlkeld came to him, and making him a sign not to rise, said aloud, 'Good Gaffer, let me see what ails thy leg.' Then kneeling down and busying herself with the bandages, she looked up piteously in his face, with the partly breathed inquiry, 'My son?'

'Well, my lady, and grown into a stalwart lad,' was Hob's answer, with an eye on the door, and in a voice as low as his gruff tones wouldpermit.

'And wherefore? What is it?' she asked anxiously. 'Be they on the track of my poor boy?'

'They may be,' answered Hob, 'wherefore I deemed it well to shift our quarters. As hap would have it, the lad fell upon a little wench lost in the mosses, and there was nothing for it but to bring her home for the night. I would have had her away as soon as day dawned, and no questions asked, but the witches, or the foul fiend himself, must needs bring up a snow-storm, and there was nothing for it but to let her bide in the cot all day, giving tongue as none but womenfolk can do; and behold she is the child of the Lord St. John of Bletso.'

'Nay, what should bring her north?'

'She wonnes at Greystone with the wild Prioress Selby, who lost her out hawking. Her father is a black Yorkist. I saw him up to his stirrups in blood at St. Albans!'

'But sure my boy did not make himself known to her?' exclaimed the lady.

'I trow not. He has been well warned, and is a lad of his word; but the two bairns, left to themselves, could scarce help finding out that each was of gentle blood and breeding, and how much more my goodwife cannot tell. I took the maid back so soon as it was safe yester morn, and sent back my young lord, much against his will, half-way to Greystone. And well was it I did so, for he was scarce over the ridge when a plump of spears came in sight on the search for him, and led by the young squire of Selby.'

'Ah! and if the damsel does but talk, even if she knows nought, the foe will draw their conclusions!' said the lady, clasping her hands. 'Oh, would that I had sent him abroad with his little brothers!'

'Nay, then might he have fallen into the hands of Bletso himself, and they say Burgundy is all for the Yorkists now,' said Hob. 'This is what I have done, gracious lady. I bade my good woman carry off all she could from the homestead and burn the rest; and for him we wot on, I sent him and his flock off westward, appointing each of them the same trysting-place—on the slope beneath Derwent Hill, my lady—whence I thought, if it were your will and the good knight Sir Lancelot's, we might go nigher to the sea and the firth, where the Selby clan have no call, being at deadly feud with the Ridleys. So if the maiden's tongue goes fast, and the Prioress follows up the quest with young Selby, they will find nought for their pains.'

'Thou art a good guardian, Hob! Ah! where would my boy be save for thee? And thou sayest he is even now at the very border of the forest ground! Sure, there can be no cause that I should not go and see him. My heart hungers for my children. Oh, let me go with thee!'

'Sir Lancelot—' began Hob.

'He is away at the Warden's summons. He will scarce be back for a week or more. I will, I must go with thee, good Hob.'

'Not in your own person, good madam,' stipulated Hob. 'As thou knowest, there are those in Sir Lancelot's following who might be too apt to report of secret visits, and that were as ill as the Priory folk.'

It was then decided that the lady should put on the disguise of a countrywoman bringing eggs and meat to sell at the castle, and meet Hob near the postern, whence a path led to Penrith.

Hob, having received a lump of oatcake and a draught of very small ale, limped out of the court, and, so soon as he could find a convenient spot behind the gorse bushes, divested himself of his bandages, and changed the side of his shepherd's plaid to one much older and more weather-beaten; also his pilgrim's hat for one in his pouch—a blue bonnet, more like the national Scottish head-gear, hiding the hat in the gorse.

Then he lay down and waited, where he could see a window, whence a red kerchief was to be fluttered to show when the lady would be ready for him to attend her. He waited long, for she had first to disarm suspicion by presiding at the general meal of the household, and showing no undue haste.

At last, though not till after he had more than once fallen asleep and feared that he had missed the signal, or that his wife and 'Hal' might be tempted to some imprudence while waiting, he beheld the kerchief waving in the sunset light of the afternoon, and presently, shrouded in such a black and white shepherd's maud as his own, and in a russet gown with a basket on her arm, his lady came forth and joined him.

His first thought was how would she return again, when the darkness was begun, but her only answer was, 'Heed not that! My child, I must see.'

Indeed, she was almost too breathless and eager with haste, as he guided her over the rough and difficult path, or rather track, to answer his inquiries as to what was to be done next. Her view, however, agreed with his, that they must lurk in the borders of the woodland for a day or two till Sir Lancelot's return, when he would direct them to a place where he could put them under the protection of one of the tenants of his manor. It was a long walk, longer than Hob had perhaps felt when he had undertaken to conduct the lady through it, for ladies, though inured to many dangers in those days, were unaccustomed to travelling on their own feet; but the mother's heart seemed to heed no obstacle, though moments came when she had to lean heavily on her companion, and he even had to lift her over brooks or pools; but happily the sun had not set when they made their way through the tangles of the wood, and at last saw before them the fitful glow of a fire of dead leaves, branches and twigs, while the bark of a dog greeted the rustling, they made.

'Sweetheart, my faithful!' then shouted Hob, and in another moment there was a cry, 'Ha! Halloa! Master Hob—beest there?'

'His voice!—my son's!' gasped the lady, and sank for a moment of overwhelming joy against the faithful retainer, while the shaggy dog leapt upon them both.

'Ay, lad, here—and some one else.'

The boy crashed through the underwood, and stood on the path in a moment's hesitation. Mother and son were face to face!

The years that had passed had changed the lad from almost a babe into a well-grown strong boy but the mother was little altered, and as she held out her arms no word was wasted ere he sprang into them, and his face was hidden on her neck as when he knew his way into her embrace of old!

When the intense rapturous hold was loosed they were aware of Goodwife Dolly looking on with clasped hands and streaming eyes, giving thanks for the meeting of her dear lady and the charge whom she and her husband had so faithfully kept.

When the mother and son had leisure to look round, and there was a pleased survey of the boy's height and strength, Goodwife Dolly came forward to beg the lady to come to her fire, and rest under the gipsy tent which she and nephew Piers—her *real* herd-boy, a rough, shaggy, almost dumb and imbecile lad—had raised with branches, skins and canvas, to protect their few articles of property. There was a smouldering fire, over which Doll had prepared a rabbit which the dog had caught, and which she had intended for Hal's supper and that of her husband if he came home in time. While the lady lavished thanks upon her for all she had done for the boy she was intent on improving the rude meal, so as to strengthen her mistress after her long walk, and for the return. The lady, however, could see and think of nothing but her son, while he returned her tearful gaze with open eyes, gathering up his old recollections of her.

'Mother!' he said—with a half-wondering tone, as the recollections of six years old came back to him more fully, and then he nestled again in her arms as if she were far more real to him than at first—'Mother!' And then, as she sobbed over him, 'The little one?'

'The babe is well, when last I heard of her, in a convent at York. Thou rememberest her?'

'Ay—my little sister! Ay,' he said, with a considering interrogative sound, 'I mind her well, and old Bunce too, that taught me to ride.'

But Hob interrupted the reminiscences by bringing up the pony on which

Anne had ridden, and insisting that the lady should not tarry longer. 'He,' indicating Hal, might walk beside her through the wood, and thus prolong their interview, but, as she well knew, it was entirely unsafe to remain any longer away from the castle.

There were embraces and sobbing thanks exchanged between the lady and her son's old nurse, and then Hal, at a growling hint from Hob, came forward, and awkwardly helped her to her saddle. He walked by her side through the wood, holding her rein, while Hob, going before, did his best in the twilight to clear away the tangled branches and brambles that fell across the path, and were near of striking the lady across the face as she rode.

On the way she talked to her son about his remembrances, anxious to know how far his dim recollections went of the old paternal castle in Bedfordshire, of his infant sister and brother, and his father. Of him he had little recollection, only of being lifted in his arms, kissed and blessed, and seeing him ride away with his troop, clanking in their armour. After that he remembered nothing, save the being put into a homelier dress, and travelling on Nurse Dolly's lap in a wain, up and down, it seemed to him, for ever, till at last clearer recollections awoke in him, and he knew himself as Hal the shepherd's boy, with the sheep around him, and the blue starry sky above him.

'Dost thou remember what thou wast called in those times?' asked his mother.

'I was always Hal. The little one was Meg,' he said.

'Even so, my boy, my dear boy! But knowst thou no more than this?'

'Methinks, methinks there were serving-men that called me the young Lord. Ay, so! But nurse said I must forget all that. Mother dear, when that maiden came and talked of tilts and lances, meseemed that I recollected somewhat. Was then my father a knight?'

'Alack! alack! my child, that thou shouldst not know!'

'Memories came back with that maiden's voice and thine,' said Hal, in a bewildered tone. 'My father! Was he then slain when he rode farther?'

'Ah! I may tell thee now thou art old enough to guard thyself,' she said. 'Thy father, whom our blessed Lord assoilzie, was the Lord Clifford, slain by savage hands on Towton field for his faith to King Harry! Thou, my poor boy, art the Baron of Clifford, though while this cruel House of York be in power thou must keep in hiding from them in this mean disguise. Woe worth the day!'

'And am I then a baron—a lord?' said the boy. 'Great lords have books.

Were there not some big ones on the hall window seats? Did not Brother Eldred begin to teach me my letters? I would that I could go on to learn more!'

'Oh, I would that thou couldst have all knightly training, and learn to use sword and lance like thy gallant father!'

'Nay, but I saw a poor man fall off his horse and lie hurt, I do not want those hard, cruel ways. And my father was slain. Must a lord go to battle?'

'Boy, boy, thou wilt not belie thy Clifford blood,' cried the lady in consternation, which was increased when he said, 'I have no mind to go out and kill folks or be killed. I had rather mark the stars and tend my sheep.'

'Alack! alack! This comes of keeping company with the sheep. That my son, and my lord's son, should be infected with their sheepish nature!'

'Never fear, madam,' said Hob. 'When occasion comes, and strength is grown, his blood will show itself.'

'If I could only give him knightly breeding!' sighed the lady. 'Sir Lancelot may find the way. I cannot see him grow up a mere shepherd boy.'

'Content you, madam,' said Hob. 'Never did I see a shepherd boy with the wisdom and the thought there is in that curly pate!'

'Wisdom! thought!' muttered the lady. 'Those did not save our good King, only made him a saint. I had rather hear the boy talk of sword and lance than prate of books and stars! And that wench, whom to our misfortune thou didst find! What didst tell her?'

'I told her nought, mother, for I had nought to tell.'

'She scented mystery, though,' said Hob. 'She saw he was no herd boy.'

'Nay? Though he holds himself like a lout untrained! Would that I could have thee in hand, my son, to make thee meet to tread in thy brave father's steps! But now, comrade of sheep thou art, and I fear me thou wilt ever be! But that maid, I trust that she perceived nothing in thy bearing or speech?'

'She will not betray whatever she perceived,' said Hal stoutly.

The wood was by this time nearly past, and the moment of parting had come. The lady had decided on going on foot to the little grey stone church whose low square tower could be seen rising like another rock. Thither she could repair in her plaid, and by-and-by throw it off, and return in her own character to the castle, as though she had gone forth to worship there. When lifted off the shaggy pony she threw her arms round Hal, kissed him passionately, and bade him never breathe a word of it, but never to forget that a baron he was, and bound to be a good brave knight, fit to avenge his father's death!

Hal came to understand from Dolly's explanations that his recent abode had been on the estate of his grandfather, Baron de Vesci, at Londesborough, but his mother had since married Sir Lancelot Threlkeld, and had intimated that her boy should be removed thither as soon as might be expedient, and therefore the house on the Yorkshire moor had been broken up.

CHAPTER VI. — A CAUTIOUS STEPFATHER

```
Thou tree of covert and of rest
   For this young bird that was distrest.
   —WORDSWORTH.
```

A baron—bound to be a good knight, and to avenge my father's death! What does it all mean?' murmured Hal to himself as he lay on his back in the morning sunshine, on the hill-side, the wood behind him, and before him a distance of undulating ground, ending in the straight mysterious blue-grey line that Hob Hogward had told him was the sea.

'Baron! Lord Clifford, like my father! He was a man in steel armour; I remember how it rang, and how his gorget—yes, that was the thing round his throat—how it hurt me when he lifted me up to kiss me, and how they blamed me for crying out. Ay, and he lived in a castle with dark, dull, narrow chambers, all save the hall, where there was ever a tramping and a clamouring, and smells of hot burning meat, and horses, and all sorts of things, and they sat and sat over their meat and wine, and drank health to King Harry and the Red Rose. I mind now how they shouted and roared, and how I wanted to go and hide on the stairs, and my father would have me shout with them, and drink confusion to York out of his cup, and shook me and cuffed me when I cried. Oh! must one be like that to be a knight? I had rather live on these free green hills with the clear blue sky above me, and my good old ewe for my comrade'—and he fell to caressing the face of an old sheep which had come up to him, a white, mountain-bleached sheep with fine and delicate limbs. 'Yes, I love thee, good, gentle, little cwe, and thee, faithful Watch,' as a young collie pressed up to him, thrusting a long nose into his hand, 'far better than those great baying hounds, or the fierce-eyed hawks that only want to kill. If I be a baron, must it be in that sort? Avenge! avenge! what does that mean? Is it, as in Goodwife Dolly's ballads, going forth to kill? Why should I? I had rather let them be! Hark! Yea, Watch,' as the dog pricked his ears and raised his graceful head, then sprang up and uttered a deep- mouthed bark. The sheep darted away to her companions, and Hal rose to his feet, as the dog began to wave his tail, and Hob came forward accompanied by a tall, grave-looking gentleman. 'Here he be, sir. Hal, come thou and ask the blessing of thy knightly stepfather.'

Hal obeyed the summons, and coming forward put a knee to the ground, while Sir Lancelot Threlkeld uttered the conventional blessing, adding, 'Fair son, I am glad to see thee. Would that we might be better acquainted, but I fear it is not safe for thee to come and be trained for knighthood in my poor house. Thou art a well grown lad, I rejoice to see, and strong and hearty I have no doubt.'

'Ay, sir, he is strong enow, I wis; we have done our best for him,' responded Hob, while Hal stood shy and shamefaced; but there was something about his bearing that made Sir Lancelot observe, 'Ay, ay, he shows what he comes of more than his mother made me fear. Only thou must not slouch, my fair son. Raise thy head more. Put thy shoulders back. So! so! Nay.'

Poor Hal tried to obey, the colour mounting in his face, but he only became more and more stiff when he tried to be upright, and his expression was such that Sir Lancelot cried out, 'Put not on the visage of one of thine own sheep! Ah! how shalt thou be trained to be a worthy knight? I cannot take thee to mine house, for I have men there who might inform King Edward that thy mother harboured thee. And unless I could first make interest with Montagu or Salisbury, that would be thy death, if not mine.'

The boy had nothing to say to this, and stood shy by, while his stepfather explained his designs to Hal. It was needful to remove the young Baron as far as possible from the suspicion of the greater part of Sir Lancelot Threlkeld's household, and the present resting-place, within a walk of his castle, was therefore unsafe; besides that, freebooters might be another danger, so near the outskirts of the wood, since the northern districts of moor and wood were by no means clear of the remnants of the contending armies, people who were generally of the party opposite to that which they intended to rob.

But on the banks of the Derwent, not far from its fall into the sea, Sir Lancelot had granted a tenure to an old retainer of the De Vescis, who had followed his mistress in her misfortunes; and on his lands Hob Hogward might be established as a guardian of the herds with his family, which would excite no suspicion. Moreover, he could train the young Baron in martial exercises, the only other way of fitting him for his station unless he could be sent to France or Burgundy like his brother; but besides that the journey was a difficulty, it was always uncertain whether there would be revengeful exiles of one or other side in the service of their King, who might wreak the wrongs of their party on Clifford's eldest son. There was reported to be a hermit on the coast, who, if he was a scholar, might teach the young gentleman. To Sir Lancelot's surprise, his stepson's face lighted up more at this suggestion than at that of being trained in arms.

Hob had done nothing in that way, not even begun to teach him the quarterstaff, though he avouched that when there was cause the young lord was no craven, no more than any Clifford ever was—witness when he drove off the great hound, which some said was a wolf, when it fell upon the flock, or when none could hold him from climbing down the Giant's Cliff after the lamb that had fallen. No fear but he had heart enough to make his hand keep his own or other folks' heads.

'That is well,' said Sir Lancelot, looking at the lad, who stood twisting his hands in the speechless silence induced by being the subject of discussion; 'but it would be better, as my lady saith, if he could only learn not to bear himself so like a clown.'

However, there was no more time, for Simon Bunce, the old man-at-arms whom Sir Lancelot had appointed to meet him there, came in sight through the trees, riding an old grey war-horse, much resembling himself in the battered and yet strong and effective air of both. Springing down, the old man bent very low before the young Baron, raising his cap as he gave thanks to Heaven for permitting him to see his master's son. Then, after obeisance to his present master, he and Hob eagerly shook hands as old comrades and fellow-soldiers who had thought never to meet again.

Then turning again to the young noble, he poured out his love, devotion and gratitude for being able to serve his beloved lord's noble son; while poor Hal stood under the discomfort of being surrounded with friends who knew exactly what to say and do to him, their superior, while he himself was entirely at a loss how to show himself gracious or grateful as he knew he ought to do. It was a relief when Sir Lancelot said 'Enough, good Simon! Forget his nobility for the present while he goes with thee to Derwentside as herd boy to Halbert Halstead here; only thou must forget both their names, and know them only as Hal and Hob.'

With a gesture of obedience, Simon listened to the further directions, and how he was to explain that these south country folks had been sent up in charge of an especial flock of my lady's which she wished to have on the comparatively sheltered valley of the Derwent. Perhaps further directions as to the training of the young Baron were added later, but Hal did not hear them. He was glad to be dismissed to find Piers and gather the sheep together in preparation for the journey to their new quarters. Yet he did not fail to hear the sigh with which his stepfather noted that his parting salutation was far too much in the character of the herd boy.

CHAPTER VII. — ON DERWENT BANKS

When under cloud of fear he lay
  A shepherd clad in homely grey.
  —WORDSWORTH.

Simon Bunce came himself to conduct his new tenants to their abode. It was a pleasant spot, a ravine, down which the clear stream rushed on its course to mingle its waters with those of the ocean. The rocks and brushwood veiled the approach to an open glade where stood a rude stone hovel, rough enough, but possessing two rooms, a hearth and a chimney, and thus superior to the hut that had been left on the moor. There were sheds for the cattle around, and the grass was fresh and green so that the sheep, the goat and the cow began eagerly feeding, as did the pony which Hal and Piers were unloading.

On one side stretched the open moor rising into the purple hills, just touched with snow. On the other was the wooded valley of the Derwent, growing wider ever before it debouched amid rocks into the sea. The goodwife at once discovered that there had been recent habitation, and asked what had become of the former dwellers there.

'The woman fretted for company,' said Simon, 'and vowed she was in fear of the Scots, so I even let her have her way and go down to the town.'

The town in north country parlance only meant a small village, and Hob asked where it lay.

It was near the junction of the two streams, where Simon lived himself in a slightly fortified farmhouse, just high up enough to be fairly safe from flood tides. He did not advise his newly arrived tenants to be much seen at this place, where there were people who might talk. They were almost able to provide for their daily needs themselves, excepting for meal and for ale, and he would himself see to this being supplied from a more distant farm on the coast, which Hob and Piers might visit from time to time with the pony.

Goodwife Dolly inquired whether they might safely go to church, from which she had been debarred all the time they had been on the move. 'So ill for both us and the lad,' she said.

Simon looked doubtful. 'If thou canst not save thy soul without,' he said, 'thou mightst go on some feast day, when there is such a concourse of folk that thou mightst not be noticed, and come away at once without halting for idle clavers, as they call them here.'

'That's what the women folk are keen for with their church-going,' said

Hob with a grin.

'Now, husband, thou knowst,' said Dolly, injured, though she was more than aware he spoke with intent to tease her. 'Have I not lived all this while with none to speak to save thee and the blessed lads, and never murmured.'

'Though thy tongue be sore for want of speech!' laughed Hob, 'thou beest a good wife, Dolly, and maybe thy faithfulness will tell as much in the saving of thy soul as going to church.'

'Nay, but,' said Hal with eagerness, 'is there not a priest?'

'The priest comes of a White Rose house—I trust not him. Ay, goodwife, beware of showing thyself to him. I give him my dues, that he may have no occasion against me or Sir Lancelot, but I would not have him pry into knowledge that concerns him not.'

'Did not Sir Lancelot say somewhat of a scholarly hermit who might learn me in what I ought to know?' asked the boy.

'Never you fear, sir! Here are Hob Halstead and I, able to train any young noble in what behoves him most to know.'

'Yea, in arms and sports. They must be learnt I know, but a noble needs booklore too,' said the boy. 'Cannot this same hermit help me? Sir Lancelot —'

Simon Bunce interrupted sharply. 'Sir Lancelot knows nought of the hermit! He is—he is—a holy man.'

'A priest,' broke in Dolly, 'a priest!'

'No such thing, dame, no clerk at all, I tell thee. And ye lads had best not molest him! He is for ever busy with his prayers, and wants none near him.'

Hal was disappointed, for his mind was far less set on the exercises of a young knight than on the desire to acquire knowledge, that study which seemed to be thrown away on the unwilling ears of Anne St. John.

Hob had been awakened by contact with his lady and her husband, as well as with the old comrade, Simon Bunce, to perceive that if there were any chance of the young Lord Clifford's recovering his true position he must not be allowed to lounge and slouch about like Piers, and he was continually calling him to order, making him sit and stand upright, as he had seen the young pages forced to do at the castle, learn how to handle a sword, and use the long stick which was the substitute for a lance, and to mount and sit on the old pony as a knight should do, till poor Hal had no peace, and was glad to get away upon the moor with Piers and the sheep, where there was no one to criticise him, or predict that nothing would ever make him do honour to his name if he were proved ten times a baron.

It was still worse when Bunce came over, and brought a taller horse, and such real weapons as he deemed that the young lord might be taught to use, and there were doleful auguries and sharp reproofs, designed in comically respectful phrases, till he was almost beside himself with being thus tormented, and ready to wish never to hear of being a baron.

His relief was to wander away upon the moors, watch the lights and shadows on the wondrous mountains, or dream on the banks of the river, by which he could make his way to the seashore, a place of endless wonder and contemplation, as he marvelled why the waters flowed in and retreated again, watched the white crests, and the glassy rolls of the waves, felt his mind and aspiration stretched as by something illimitable, even as when he looked up to the sky, and saw star beyond star, differing from one another in brightness. There were those white birds too, differing from all the night-jars and plovers he had seen on the moor, floating now over the waves, now up aloft and away, as if they were soaring into the very skies. Oh, would that he could follow them, and rise with them to know what were those great grey or white clouds, and what was above or below in those blue vastnesses! And whence came all those strange things that the water spread at his feet the long, brown, wet streamers, or the delicate red tracery that could be seen in the clear pools, where were sometimes those lumps like raw flesh when closed, but which opened into flowers? Or the things like the snails on the heath, yet not snails, and all the strange creatures that hopped and danced in the water?

Why would no one explain such things to him? Nay, what a pity everyone treated it as mere childish folly in him to be thus interested! They did not quite dare to beat him for it—that was one use of being a baron. Indeed, one day when Simon Bunce struck him sharply and hard over the shoulders for dragging home a great piece of sea-weed with numerous curious creatures upon it, Goodwife Dolly rushed out and made such an outcry that the esquire was fain to excuse himself by declaring that it was time that my lord should know how to bide a buffet, and answer it. He was ready and glad to meet the stroke in return! 'Come on, sir!'

And Hob put a stout headless lance in the boy's hand, while Simon stood up straight before him. Hob adjusted the weapon in his inert hand, and told him how and where to strike. But 'It is not in sooth. I don't want to hurt Master Simon,' said the child, as they laughed, and yet with displeasure as his blow fell weak and uncertain.

'Is it a mouse's tail?' cried Simon in derision.

'Come, sir, try again,' said Hob. 'Strike as you did when the black bull came down. Why cannot you do the like now, when you are tingling from Bunce's stroke?'

'Ah! then I thought the bull would fall on Piers,' said Hal.

'Come on, think so now, sir. One blow to do my heart good, and show you have the arm of your forebears.'

Thus incited, with Hob calling out to him to take heart of grace, while Simon made a feint of trying to beat Mother Dolly, Hal started forward and dealt a blow sufficient to make Simon cry out, 'Ha, well struck, sir, if you had had a better grip of your lance! I even feel it through my buffcoat.'

He spoke as though it had been a kiss; but oh! and alack! why were these rough and dreary exercises all that these guardians—yea, and even Sir Lancelot and his mother—thought worth his learning, when there was so much more that awoke his delight and interest? Was it really childish to heed these things? Yet even to his young, undeveloped brain it seemed as if there must be mysteries in sky and sea, the unravelling of which would make life more worth having than the giving and taking of blows, which was all they heeded.

CHAPTER VIII. — THE HERMIT

No hermit e'er so welcome crost
  A child's lone path in woodland lost.
  —KEBLE.

Hal had wandered farther than his wont, rather hoping to be out of call if Simon arrived to give him a lesson in chivalrous sports. He found himself on the slope of one of the gorges down which smaller streams rushed in wet weather to join the Derwent. There was a sound of tinkling water, and leaning forward, Hal saw that a tiny thread of water dropped between the ferns and the stones. Therewith a low, soft chant in a manly voice, mingling with the drip of the water.

The words were strange to him&&

Lucis Creator optime,
  Lucem dierum proferens&&

but they were very sweet, and in leaning forward to look between the rowan branches and hear and see more, his foot slipped, and with Watch barking round him, he rolled helplessly down the rock, and found himself before a tall light-haired man, in a dark dress, who gave a hand to raise him, asking kindly, 'Art hurt, my child?'

'Oh, no, sir! Off, off, Watch!' as the dog was about to resent anyone's touching his master. 'Holy sir, thanks, great thanks,' as a long fair hand helped him to his feet, and brushed his soiled garment.

'Unhurt, I see,' said that sweet voice. 'Hast thou lost thy way? Good dog, thou lovest thy master! Art thou astray?'

'No, sir, thank you, I know my way home.'

'Thou art the boy who lives with the shepherd at Derwentside, on Bunce's ground?'

'Ay, Hob Hogward's herd boy,' said Hal. 'Oh, sir, are you the holy hermit of the Derwent vale?'

'A hermit for the nonce I am,' was the answer, with something of a smile responsive to the eager face.

'Oh, sir, if you be not too holy to look at me or speak to me! If you would help me to some better knowledge—not only of sword and single-stick!'

'Better knowledge, my child! Of thy God?' said the hermit, a sweet look of joy spreading over his face.

'Goodwife Dolly has told me of Him, and taught me my Pater and Credo, but we have lived far off, and she has not been able to go to church for weeks and years. But what I long after is to tell me what means all this—yonder sea, and all the stars up above. And they will call me a simpleton for marking such as these, and only want me to heed how to shoot an arrow, or give a stroke hard enough to hurt another. Do such rude doings alone, fit for a bull or a ram as meseems, go to the making of a knight, fair sir?'

'They go to the knight's keeping of his own, for others whom he ought to defend,' said the hermit sadly; 'I would have thee learn and practise them. But for the rest, thou knowest, sure, who made the stars?'

'Oh yes! Nurse Dolly told me. She saw it all in a mystery play long long ago—when a Hand came out, and put in the stars and sun and moon.'

'Knowest thou whose Hand was figured there, my child?'

'The Hand of God,' said Hal, removing his cap. 'They be sparks to show His glory! But why do some move about among the others—one big one moves from the Bull's face one winter to half-way beyond it. And is the morning star the evening one?'

'Ah! thou shouldst know Ptolemy and the Almagest,' said the hermit smiling, 'to understand the circuits of those wandering stars—Coeli enarrant gloriam Dei.'

'That is Latin,' said the boy, startled. 'Are you a priest, sir?'

'No, not I—I am not worthy,' was the answer, 'but in some things I may aid thee, and I shall be blessed in so doing. Canst say thy prayers?'

'Oh, yes! nurse makes me say them when I lie down and when I get up—Credo and Pater. She says the old parson used to teach them our own tongue for them, but she has well-nigh forgot. Can you tell me, holy man?'

'That will I, with all my heart,' responded the hermit, laying his long delicate hand on Hal's head. 'Blessed be He who has sent thee to me!'

The boy sat at the hermit's feet, listening with the eagerness of one whose soul and mind had alike been under starvation, and how time went neither knew till there was a rustling and a step. Watch sprang up, but in another moment Simon Bunce, cap in hand, stood before the hut, beginning with 'How now, sir?'

The hermit raised his hand, as if to make a sign, saying, 'Thou seest I have a guest, good friend.'

Bunce started back with 'Oh! the young Lord! Sworn to silence, I trust! I bade him not meddle with you, sir.'

'It was against his will, I trow,' said the hermit. 'He fell over the rock by the waterfall, but since he is here, I will answer for him that he does no hurt by word or deed!'

'Never, holy sir!' eagerly exclaimed Hal. 'Hob Hogward knows that I can keep my mouth shut. And may I come again?'

Simon was shaking his head, but the hermit took on him to say, 'Gladly will I welcome thee, my fair child, whensoever thou canst find thy way to the weary old anchoret! Go thy way now! Or hast thou lost it?'

'No, sir; I ken the woodland and can soon be at home,' replied Hal; then, putting a knee to the ground, 'May I have your blessing, holy man?'

'Alack, I told thee I am no priest,' said the hermit; 'but for such as I am, I bless thee with all my soul, thou fatherless lad,' and he laid his hand on the young lad's wondering brow, then bade him begone, since Simon and himself had much to say to one another.

Hal summoned Watch, and turned to a path through the wood, leading towards the coast, wondering as he walked how the hermit seemed to know him—him whose presence had been so sedulously concealed. Could it be that so very holy a man had something of the spirit of prophecy?

He kept his promise of silence, and indeed his guardians were so much accustomed to his long wanderings that he encountered no questions, only one of Hob's growls that he should always steal away whenever there was a chance of Master Bunce's coming to try to make a man of him.

However, Bunce himself arrived shortly after, and informed Hob that since young folks always pried where they were least wanted, and my lord had stumbled incontinently on the anchoret's den, it was the holy man's will that he might come there whenever he chose. A pity and shame it was, but it would make him more than ever a mere priestling, ever hankering after books and trash!

'Were it not better to ask my lady and Sir Lancelot if they would have it so? I could walk over to Threlkeld!'

'No, no, no, on your life not,' exclaimed Simon, striking his staff on the ground in his vehemence. 'Never a word to the Threlkeld or any of his kin! Let well alone! I only wish the lad had never gone a-roaming there! But holy men must not be gainsaid, even if it does make a poor craven scholar out of his father's son.'

And thus began a time of great contentment to the Lord Clifford. There were few days on which he did not visit the hermitage. It was a small log hut, but raised with some care, and made weatherproof with moss and clay in the crevices, and there was an inner apartment, with a little oil lamp burning before a rough wooden cross, where Hal, if the hermit were not outside, was certain to find him saying his prayers. Food was supplied by Simon himself, and, since Hal's admission, was often carried by him, and the hermit seemed to spend his time either in prayer or in a gentle dreamy state of meditation, though he always lighted up into animation at the arrival of the boy whom he had made his friend. Hal had thought him old at first, on the presumption that all hermits must be aged, nor was it likely that age should be estimated by one living such a life, but the light hair, untouched with grey, the smooth cheeks and the graceful figure did not belong to more than a year or two above forty. And he had no air of ill health, yet this calm solitary residence in the wooded valley seemed to be infinite rest to him.

Hal had no knowledge nor experience to make him wonder, and accepted the great quiet and calm of the hermit as the token of his extreme holiness and power of meditation. He himself was always made welcome with Watch by his side, and encouraged to talk and ask questions, which the hermit answered with what seemed to the boy the utmost wisdom, but older heads would have seen not to be that of a clever man, but of one who had been fairly educated for the time, had had experience of courts and camps, and referred all the inquiries and wonderments which were far beyond him direct to Almighty Power.

The mind of the boy advanced much in this intercourse with the first cultivated person he had encountered, and who made a point of actually teaching and explaining to him all those mysteries of religion which poor old Dolly only blindly accepted and imparted as blindly to her nursling. Of actual instruction, nothing was attempted. A little portuary, or abbreviated manual of the service, was all that the hermit possessed, treasured with his small crucifix in his bosom, and of course it was in Latin. The Hours of the Church he knew by heart, and never failed to observe them, training his young pupil in the repetition and English meaning of such as occurred during his visits. He also told much of the history of the world, as he knew it, and of the Church and the saints, to the eager mind that absorbed everything and reflected on it, coming with fresh questions that would have been too deep and perplexing for his friend if he had not always determined everything with 'Such is the will of God.'

Somewhat to the surprise of Simon Bunce and Hob Hogward, Hal improved greatly, not only in speech but in bearing; he showed no such dislike or backwardness in chivalrous exercises as previously; and when once Sir Lancelot Threlkeld came over to see him, he was absolutely congratulated on looking so much more like a young knight.

'Ay,' said Bunce, taking all the merit to himself, 'there's noughtlike having an old squire trained in the wars in France to show a stripling how to hold a lance.'

Hal had been too well tutored to utter a word of him to whom his improvement was really due, not by actual training, but partly by unconscious example in dignified grace and courtesy of demeanour, and partly by the rather sad assurances that it was well that a man born to his station, if he ever regained it, should be able to defend himself and others, and not be a helpless burthen on their hands. Tales of the Seven Champions of Christendom and of King Arthur and his Knights likewise had their share in the moulding of the youthful Lord Clifford.

His great desire was to learn to read, but it was not encouraged by the hermit, nor was there any book available save the portuary, crookedly and contractedly written on vellum, so as to be illegible to anyone unfamiliar with writing, with Latin, or the service. However, the anchoret yielded to his importunity so far as to let him learn the alphabet, traced on the door in charcoal, and identify the more sacred words in the book—which, indeed, were all in gold, red and blue.

He did not advance more than this, for his teacher was apt to go off in a musing dream of meditation, repeating over and over in low sweet tones the holy phrases, and not always rousing himself when his pupil made a remark or asked a question. Yet he was always concerned at his own inattention when awakened, and would apologise in a tone of humility that always made Hal feel grieved and ashamed of having been importunate. For there was a dignity and gentleness about the hermit that always made the boy feel the contrast with his own roughness and uncouthness, and reverence him as something from a holier world.

'Nurse, I do think he is a saint,' one day said Hal.

'Nay, nay, my laddie, saints don't come down from heaven in these days of evil.'

'I would thou could see him when one comes upon him at his prayers. His face is like the angel at the cross I saw so long ago in the castle chapel.'

'Dost thou remember that chapel? Thou wert a babe when we quitted it.'

'I had well nigh forgotten it, but the good hermit's face brought all back again, and the voice of the father when he said the Service.'

'That thou shouldst mind so long! This hermit is no priest, thou sayst?'

'No, he said he was not worthy; but sure all saints were not priests, nurse.'

'Nay, it is easy to be more worthy than the Jack Priests I have known. Though I would they would let me go to church. But look thee here, Hal, if he be such a saint as thou sayst, maybe thou couldst get him to bestow a blessing on poor Piers, and give him his hearing and voice.'

Hal was sure that his own special saint was holy enough for anything, and accordingly asked permission of him to bring his silent companion for blessing and healing.

The mild blue eye lighted for a moment. 'Is the poor child then afflicted with the King's Evil?' the hermit asked.

'Nay, he is sound enough in skin and limb. It is that he can neither hear nor speak, and if you, holy sir, would lay thine hand on him, and sign him with the rood, and pray, mayhap your holiness—'

'Peace, peace,' cried the hermit impetuously, lifting up his hand. 'Dost not know that I am a sinner like unto the rest—nay, a greater sinner, in that a burthen was laid on me that I had not the soul to rise to, so that the sin and wickedness of thousands have been caused by my craven faint heart for well nigh two score years? O miserere Domine.'

He threw himself on the ground with clasped hands, and Hal, standing by in awestruck amazement, heard no more save sobs, mingled with the supplications of the fifty-first Psalm.

He was obliged at last to go away without having been able to recall the attention of his friend from his agony of prayer. With the reticence that had grown upon him, he did not mention at home the full effect of his request, but when he thought it over he was all the more convinced that his friend was a great saint. Had he not always heard that saints believed themselves great sinners, and went through many penances? And why did he speak as if he could have cured the King's Evil? He asked Dolly what it was, and she replied that it was the sickness that only the King's touch could heal.

CHAPTER IX. — HENRY OF WINDSOR

My crown is in my heart, not on my head;
  Not deck'd with diamonds, and Indian stones,
  Nor to be seen. My crown is call'd Content.
—SHAKESPEARE.

Summer had faded, and an early frost had tinted the fern-leaves with gold here and there, and made the hermit wrap himself close in a cloak lined with thick brown fur.

Simon, who was accustomed very respectfully to take the command of him, insisted that he should have a fire always burning on a rock close to his door, and that Piers, if not Hal, should always take care that it never went out, smothering it with peat, as every shepherd boy knew how to do, so as to keep it alight, or, in case of need, to conceal it with turf.

One afternoon, as Hal lay on the grass, whiling away the time by alternately playing with Watch and trying to unravel the mysteries of a flower of golden-rod, until the hermit should have finished his prayers and be ready to attend to him, Piers came through the wood, evidently sent on a message, and made him understand that he was immediately wanted at home.

Hal turned to take leave of his host, but the hermit's eyes were raised in such rapt contemplation as to see nought, and, indeed, it might be matter of doubt whether he had ever perceived the presence of his visitor.

Hal directed Piers to arrange the fire, and hurried away, becoming conscious as he came in sight of the cottage that there were horses standing before it, and guessing at once that it must be a visit from Sir Lancelot Threlkeld.

It was Simon Bunce, however, who, with demonstrations of looking for him, came out to meet him as he emerged from the brushwood, and said in a gruff whisper, clutching his shoulder hard, 'Not a word to give a clue! Mum! More than your life hangs on it.'

No more could pass, to explain the clue intended, whether to the presence of the young Lord Clifford himself, which was his first thought, or to the inhabitant of the hermitage. For Sir Lancelot's cheerful voice was exclaiming, 'Here he is, my lady! Here's your son! How now, my young lord? Thou hast learnt to hold up thy head! Ay, and to bow in better sort,' as, bending with due grace, Hal paused for a second ere hurrying forward to kneel before his mother, who raised him in her arms and kissed him with fervent affection. 'My son! mine own dear boy, how art thou grown! Thou hast well nigh a knightly bearing!' she exclaimed. 'Master Bunce hath done well by thee.'

'Good blood will out, my lady,' quoth Simon, well pleased at her praise.

'He hath had no training but thine?' said Sir Lancelot, looking full at Simon.

'None, Sir Knight, unless it be honest Halstead's here.'

'Methought I heard somewhat of the hermit in the glen,' put in the lady.

'He is a saint!' declared two or three voices, as if this precluded his being anything more.

'A saint,' repeated the lady. 'Anchorets are always saints. What doth he?'

'Prayeth,' answered Simon. 'Never doth a man come in but he is at his prayers. 'Tis always one hour or another!'

'Ay?' said Sir Lancelot, interrogatively. 'Sayest thou so? Is he an old man?'

Simon put in his word before Hal could speak: 'Men get so knocked about in these wars that there's no guessing their age. I myself should deem that the poor rogue had had some clouts on the head that dazed him and made him fit for nought save saying his prayers.'

Here Sir Lancelot beckoned Simon aside, and walked him away, so as to leave the mother and son alone together.

Lady Threlkeld questioned closely as to the colour of the eyes and hair, and the general appearance of the hermit, and Hal replied, without suspicion, that the eyes were blue, the hair, he thought, of a light colour, the frame tall and slight, graceful though stooping; he had thought at first that the hermit must be old, very old, but had since come to a different conclusion. His dress was a plain brown gown like a countryman's. There was nobody like him, no one whom Hal so loved and venerated, and he could not help, as he stood by his mother, pouring out to her all his feeling for the hermit, and the wise patient words that now and then dropped from him, such as 'Patience is the armour and conquest of the godly;' or, 'Shall a man complain for the punishment of his sins?' 'Yet,' said Hal, 'what sins could the anchoret have? Never did I know that a man could be so holy here on earth. I deemed that was only for the saints in heaven.'

The lady kissed the boy and said, 'I trow thou hast enjoyed a great honour, my child.'

But she did not say what it was, and when her husband summoned her, she joined him to repair to Penrith, where they were keeping an autumn retirement at a monastery, and had contrived to leave their escort and make this expedition on their way.

Simon examined Hal closely on what he had said to his mother, sighed heavily, and chided him for prating when he had been warned against it, but that was what came of dealing with children and womenfolk.

'What can be the hurt?' asked Hal. 'Sir Lancelot knows well who I am! No lack of prudence in him would put men on my track.'

'Hear him!' cried Simon; 'he thinks there is no nobler quarry in the woods than his lordship!'

'The hermit! Oh, Simon, who is he?'

But Simon began to shout for Hob Hogward, and would not hear any further questions before he rode away, as far as Hal could see, in the opposite direction to the hermitage. But when he repaired thither the next day he was startled by hearing voices and the stamp of horses, and as he reconnoitred through the trees he saw half a dozen rough-looking men, with bows and arrows, buff coats, and steel-guarded caps—outlaws and robbers as he believed.

His first thought was that they meant harm to the gentle hermit, and his impulse was to start forward to his protection or assistance, but as he sprang into sight one of the strangers cried out: 'How now! Here's a shepherd thrusting himself in. Back, lad, or 'twill be the worse for you.'

'The hermit! the hermit! Do not meddle with him! He's a saint,' shouted Hal.

But even as he spoke he became aware of Simon, who called out: 'Hold, sir; back, Giles; this is one well nigh in as much need of hiding as him yonder. Well come, since you be come, my lord, for we cannot get *him* there away without a message to you, and 'tis well he should be off ere the sleuth-hounds can get on the scent.'

'What! Where! Who?' demanded the bewildered boy, breaking off, as at that moment his friend appeared at the door of the hovel, no longer in the brown anchoret's gown but in riding gear, partially defended by slight armour, and with a cap on his head, which made him look much younger than he had before done.

'Child, art thou there? It is well; I could scarce have gone without bidding thee farewell,' he said in his sweet voice; 'thou, the dear companion of my loneliness.'

'O sir, sir, and are you going away?'

'Yea, so they will have it! These good fellows are come to guard me.'

'Oh! may I not go with thee?'

'Nay, my fair son. Thou art beneath thy mother's wing, while I am like one who was hunted as a partridge on the mountains.'

'Whither, oh whither?' gasped Hal.

'That I know not! It is in the breasts of these good men, who are charged by my brave wife to have me in their care.'

'Oh! sir, sir, what shall I do without you? You that have helped me, and taught me, and opened mine eyes to all I need to know.'

'Hush, hush; it is a better master than I could ever be that thou needest. But,' as tokens of impatience manifested themselves among the rude escort, 'take thou this,' giving him the little service-book, as he knelt to receive it, scarce knowing why. 'One day thou wilt be able to read it. Poor child! whose lot it is to be fatherless and landless for me and mine, I would I could do more for thee.'

'Oh! you have done all,' sobbed Hal.

'Nay, now, but this be our covenant, my boy! If thou, and if mine own son both come to your own, thou wilt be a true and loyal man to him, even as thy father was to me, and may God Almighty make it go better with you both.'

'I will, I will! I swear by all that is holy!' gasped Hal Clifford, with a flash of perception, as he knelt.

'Come, my liege, we have far to go ere night. No time for more parting words and sighs.'

Hal scarcely knew more except that the hands were laid on his head, and the voice he had learnt to love so well said: 'The blessing of God the Father be upon thee, thou fatherless boy, and may He reward thee sevenfold for what thy father was, who died for his faithfulness to me, a sinner! Fare thee well, my boy.'

As the hand that Hal was fervently kissing was withdrawn from him he sank upon his face, weeping as one heartbroken. He scarce heard the sounds of mounting and the trampling of feet, and when he raised his head he was alone, the woods and rocks were forsaken.

He sprang up and ran along at his utmost speed on the trampled path, but when he emerged from it he could only see a dark party, containing a horseman or two, so far on the way that it was hopeless to overtake them.

He turned back slowly to the deserted hut, and again threw himself on the ground, weeping bitterly. He knew now that his friend and master had been none other than the fugitive King, Henry of Windsor.

CHAPTER X. — THE SCHOLAR OF THE MOUNTAINS

```
Not in proud pomp nor courtly state;
  Him his own thoughts did elevate,
  Most happy in the shy recess.
—WORDSWORTH.
```

The departure of King Henry was the closing of the whole intellectual and religious world that had been opened to the young Lord Clifford. To the men of his own court, practical men of the world, there were times when poor Henry seemed almost imbecile, and no doubt his attack of melancholy insanity, the saddest of his ancestral inheritances, had shattered his powers of decision and action; but he was one who 'saw far on holy ground,' and he was a well-read man in human learning, besides having the ordinary experience of having lived in the outer world, so that in every way his companionship was delightful to a thoughtful boy, wakening to the instincts of his race.

To think of being left to the society of the sheep, of dumb Piers and his peasant parents was dreariness in the extreme to one who had begun to know something like conversation, and to have his countless questions answered, or at any rate attended to. Add to this, he had a deep personal love and reverence for his saint, long before the knowing him as his persecuted King, and thus his sorrow might well be profound, as well as rendered more acute by the terror lest his even unconscious description to his mother might have been treason!

He wept till he could weep no longer, and lay on the ground in his despair till darkness was coming on, and Piers came and pulled him up, indicating by gestures and uncouth sounds that he must go home. Goodwife Dolly was anxiously looking out for him.

'Laddie, there thou beest at last! I had begun to fear me whether the robber gang had got a hold of thee. Only Hob said he saw Master Simon with them. Have they mishandled thee, mine own lad nurse's darling? Thou lookest quite distraught.'

All Hal's answer was to hide his head in her lap and weep like a babe, though she could, with all her caresses, elicit nothing from him but that his hermit was gone. No, no, the outlaws had not hurt him, but they had taken him away, and he would never come back.

'Ay, ay, thou didst love him and he was a holy man, no doubt, but one of these days thou shalt have a true knight, and that is better for a young baron to look to than a saint fitter for Heaven than for earth! Come now, stand up and eat thy supper. Don't let Hob come in and find thee crying like a swaddled babe.'

With which worldly consolations and exhortations Goodwife Dolly brought him to rise and accept his bowl of pottage, though he could not swallow much, and soon put it aside and sought his bed.

It was not till late the next day that Simon Bunce was seen riding his rough pony over the moor. Hal repaired to him at once, with the breathless inquiry, 'Where is he?'

'In safe hands! Never you fear, sir! But best know nought.'

'O Simon, was I—? Did I do him any scathe?—I—I never knew—I only told my lady mother it was a saint.'

'Ay, ay, lad, more's the pity that he is more saint than king! If my lady guessed aught, she would be loyal as became your father's wife, and methinks she would not press you hard for fear she should be forced to be aware of the truth.'

'But Sir Lancelot?'

'As far as I can gather,' explained Simon, 'Sir Lancelot is one that hath kept well with both sides, and so is able to be a protector. But down came orders from York and his crew that King Harry is reported to be lurking in some of these moors, and the Countess Clifford being his wife, he fell under suspicion of harbouring him. Nay, there was some perilous talk in his own household, so that, as I understand the matter, he saw the need of being able to show that he knew nothing; or, if he found that the King was living within these lands, of sending him a warning ere avowing that he had been there. So I read what was said to me.'

'He knew nothing from me! Neither he nor my lady mother,' eagerly said Hal. 'When I mind me I am sure my mother cut me short when I described the hermit too closely, lest no doubt she should guess who he was.'

'Belike! It would be like my lady, who is a loyal Lancastrian at heart, though much bent on not offending her husband lest his protection should be withdrawn from you.'

'Better—O, a thousand times better!—he gave me up than the King!'

'Hush! What good would that do? A boy like you? Unless they took you in hand to make you a traitor, and offered you your lands if you would swear allegiance to King Edward, as he calls himself.'

'Never, though I were cut into quarters!' averred Hal, with a fierce gesture, clasping his staff. 'But the King? Where and what have they done with him?'

'Best not to know, my lord,' said Simon. 'In sooth, I myself do not know whither he is gone, only that he is with friends.'

'But who—what were they? They looked like outlaws!'

'So they were; many a good fellow is of Robin of Redesdale's train. There are scores of them haunting the fells and woods, all Red Rose men, keeping a watch on the King,' replied Simon. 'We had made up our minds that he had been long enough in one place, and that he must have taken shelter the winter through, when I got notice of these notions of Sir Lancelot, and forthwith sent word to them to have him away before worse came of it.'

'Oh! why did you not let me go with him? I would have saved him, waited on him, fought for him.'

'Fine fighting—when there's no getting you to handle a lance, except as if you wanted to drive a puddock with a reed! Though you have been better of late, little as your hermit seemed the man to teach you.'

'He said it was right and became a man! Would I were with him! He, my true King! Let me go to him when you know where, good Simon. I, that am his true and loving liegeman, should be with him.'

'Ay! when you are a man to keep his head and your own.'

'But I could wait on him.'

'Would you have us bested to take care of two instead of one, and my lady, moreover, in a pother about her son, and Sir Lancelot stirred to make a hue and cry all the more? No, no, sir, bide in peace in the safe homestead where you are sheltered, and learn to be a man, minding your exercises as well as may be till the time shall come.'

'When I shall be a man and a knight, and do deeds of derring-do in his cause,' cried Hal.

And the stimulus drove him on to continual calls to Hob, in Simon's default, to jousts with sword or spear, represented generally by staves; and when these could not be had, he was making arrows and practising with them, so as to become a terror to the wild ducks and other neighbours on the wolds, the great geese and strange birds that came in from the sea in the cold weather. When it was not possible to go far afield in the frosts and snows, he conned King Henry's portuary, trying to identify the written words with those he knew by heart, and sometimes trying to trace the shapes of the letters on the snow with a stick; visiting, too, the mountains and looking into the limpid grey waters of the lakes, striving hard to guess why, when the sea rose in tides, they were still. More than ever, too, did the starry skies fill him with contemplation and wonder, as he dwelt on the scraps alike of astronomy, astrology, and devotion which he had gathered from his oracle in the hermitage, and longed more and more for the time to return when he should again meet his teacher, his saint, and his King.

Alas! that time was never to come. The outlawed partisans of the Red Rose had secret communications which spread intelligence rapidly throughout the country, and long before Sir Lancelot and his lady knew, and thus it was that Simon Bunce learnt, through the outlaws, that poor King Henry had been betrayed by treachery, and seized by John Talbot at Waddington Hall in Lancashire. Deep were the curses that the outlaws uttered, and fierce were the threats against the Talbot if ever he should venture himself on the Cumbrian moors; and still hotter was their wrath, more bitter the tears of the shepherd lord, when the further tidings were received that the Earl of Warwick had brought the gentle, harmless prince, to whom he had repeatedly sworn fealty, into London with his feet tied to the stirrups of a sorry jade, and men crying before him, 'Behold the traitor!'

The very certainty that the meek and patient King would bear all with rejoicing in the shame and reproach that led him in the steps of his Master, only added to the misery of Hal as he heard the tale; and he lay on the ground before his hut, grinding his teeth with rage and longing to take revenge on Warwick, Edward, Talbot—he knew not whom—and grasping at the rocks as if they were the stones of the Tower which he longed to tear down and liberate his beloved saint.

Nor, from that time, was there any slackness in acquiring or practising all skill in chivalrous exercises.

CHAPTER XI. — THE RED ROSE

That Edward is escaped from your brother
  And fled, as he hears since, to Burgundy.
  —SHAKESPEARE.

Years passed on, and still Henry Clifford continued to be the shepherd. Matters were still too unsettled, and there were too many Yorkists in the north, keeping up the deadly hatred of the family against that of Clifford, for it to be safe for him to show himself openly. He was a tall, well-made, strong youth, and his stepfather spoke of his going to learn war in Burgundy; but not only was his mother afraid to venture him there, but he could not bear to leave England while there was a hope of working in the cause of the captive King, though the Red Rose hung withered on the branches.

Reports of misunderstandings between King Edward and the Earl of Warwick came from time to time, and that Queen Margaret and her son were busy beyond seas, which kept up hope; and in the meantime Hal grew in the knowledge of all country lore, of herd and wood, and added to it all his own earnest love of the out-of-door world, of sun, moon, and stars, sea and hills, beast and bird. The hermit King, who had been a well-educated, well-read man in his earlier days, had given him the framework of such natural science as had come down to the fifteenth century, backed by the deepest faith in scriptural descriptions; and these inferences and this philosophy were enough to lead a far acuter and more able intellect, with greater opportunities of observation, much further into the fields of the mystery of nature than ever the King had gone.

He said nothing, for never had he met one who understood a word he said apart from fortune telling, excepting the royal teacher after whom he longed; but he watched, he observed, and he dreamt, and came to conclusions that his King's namesake cousin, Enrique of Portugal, the discoverer, in his observatory at St. Vincent, might have profited by. Brother Brian, a friar, for whose fidelity Simon Bunce's outlaw could absolutely answer, and who was no Friar Tuck, in spite of his rough life, gave Dolly much comfort religiously, carried on some of the education for which Hal longed, and tried to teach him astrology. Some of the yearnings of his young soul were thus gratified, but they were the more extended as he grew nearer manhood, and many a day he stood with eyes stretched over the sea to the dim line of the horizon, with arms spread for a moment as if he would join the flight of the sea-gulls floating far, far away, then clasped over his breast in a sort of despair at being bound to one spot, then pressed the tighter in the strong purpose of fighting for his imprisoned King when the time should come.

For this he diligently practised with bow and arrow when alone, or only with Piers, and learnt all the feats of arms that Simon Runce or Giles Spearman could teach him. Spearman was evidently an accomplished knight or esquire; he had fought in France as well as in the home wars, and knew all the refinements of warfare in an age when the extreme weight of the armour rendered training and skill doubly necessary. Spearman was evidently not his real name, and it was evident that he had some knowledge of Hal's real rank, though he never hazarded mention of other name or title. The great drawback was the want of horses. The little mountain ponies did not adequately represent the warhorses trained to charge under an enormous load, and the buff jerkins and steel breast-plates of the outlaws were equally far from showing how to move under 'mail and plates of Milan steel.' Nor would Sir Lancelot Threlkeld lend or give what was needful. Indeed, he was more cautious than ever, and seemed really alarmed as well as surprised to see how tall and manly his step-son was growing, and how like his father. He would not hear of a visit to Threlkeld under any disguise, though Lady Clifford was in failing health, nor would he do anything to forward the young lord's knightly training. In effect, he only wanted to keep as quiet and unobserved as possible, for everything was in a most unsettled and dangerous condition, and there was no knowing what course was the safest for one by no means prepared to lose life or lands in any cause.

The great Earl of Warwick, on whom the fate of England had hitherto hinged, was reported to have never forgiven King Edward for his marriage with Dame Elizabeth Grey, and to be meditating insurrection. Encouraged by this there was a great rising in Yorkshire of the peasants under Robin of Redesdale, and a message was brought to Giles Spearman and his followers to join them, but he and Brother Brian demurred, and news soon came that the Marquess of Montagu had defeated the rising and beheaded Redesdale.

Sir Lancelot congratulated his step-son on having been too late to take up arms, and maintained that the only safe policy was to do nothing, a plan which suited age much better than youth.

He still lived with Hob and Piers, and slept at the hut, but he went further and further afield among the hills and mosses, often with no companion save Watch, so that he might without interruption watch the clear streams and wonder what filled their fountains, and why the sea was never full, or stand on the sea-shore studying the tides, and trying to construct a theory about them. King Henry was satisfied with 'Hitherto shalt thou come and no farther,' but He who gave that decree must have placed some cause or rule in nature thus to affect them. Could it be the moon? The waves assuredly obeyed the changes of the moon, and Hal was striving to keep a record in strokes marked by a stick on soft earth or rows of pebbles, so as to establish a rule. 'Aye, aye,' quoth Hob. 'Poor fellow, he is not much wiser than the hermit. See how he plays with pebbles and stones. You'll make nought of him, fine grown lad as he is. Why, he'll sit dazed and moonstruck half a day, and all the night, staring up at the stars as if he would count them!'

So spoke the stout shepherd to Simon Bunce, pointing to the young man, who lay at his length upon the grass calculating the proportions of the stones that marked the relations of hours of the flood tide and those of the height of the moon. Above and beyond was a sundial cut out in the turf, from his own observations after the hints that the hermit and the friar had given him.

'Ha now, my lord, I have rare news for you.'

The unwonted title did not strike Hal's unaccustomed ears, and he continued moving his lips, 'High noon, spring tide.'

'There, d'ye see?' said Hob, 'he heeds nothing. 'That I and my goodwife should have bred up a mooncalf! Here, Hal, don't you know Simon? Hear his tidings!'

'Tidings enow! King Henry is freed, King Edward is fled. My Lord of Warwick has turned against him for good and all. King Henry is proclaimed in all the market-places! I heard it with my own ears at Penrith!' And throwing up his cap into the air, while the example was followed by Hob, with 'God save King Henry, and you my Lord of Clifford.'

The sound was echoed by a burst of voices, and out of the brake suddenly stood the whole band of outlaws, headed by Giles Spearman, but Hal still stood like one dazed. 'King Harry, the hermit, free and on his throne,' he murmured, as one in a dream.

'Ay, all things be upset and reversed,' said Spearman, with a hand on his shoulder. 'No herd boy now, but my Lord of Clifford.'

'Come to his kingdom,' repeated Hal. 'My own King Harry the hermit! I would fain go and see him.'

'So you shall, my brave youth, and carry him your homage and mine,' said Spearman. 'He will know me for poor Giles Musgrave, who upheld his standard in many a bloody field. We will off to Sir Lancelot at Threlkeld now! Spite of his policy of holes and corners, he will not now refuse to own you for what you are, aye, and fit you out as becomes a knight.'

'God grant he may!' muttered Bunce, 'without his hum and ha, and swaying this way and that, till he never moves at all! Betwixt his caution, and this lad's moonstruck ways, you have a fair course before you, Sir Giles! See, what's the lad doing now?'

The lad was putting into his pouch the larger white pebbles that had represented tens in his calculation, and murmuring the numbers they stood for. 'He will understand,' he said almost to himself, but he showed himself ready to go with the party to Threlkeld, merely pausing at Hob's cottage to pick up a few needful equipments. In the skin of a rabbit, carefully prepared, and next wrapped in a silken kerchief, and kept under his chaff pillow, was the hermit's portuary, which was carefully and silently transferred by Hal to his own bosom. Sir Giles Musgrave objected to Watch, in city or camp, and Hal was obliged to leave him to Goodwife Dolly and to Piers.

With each it was a piteous parting, for Dolly had been as a mother to him for almost all his boyhood, and had supplied the tenderness that his mother's fears and Sir Lancelot's precautions had prevented his receiving at Threlkeld. He was truly as a son to her, and she sobbed over him, declaring that she never would see him again, even if he came to his own, which she did not believe was possible, and who would see to his clean shirts?

'Never fear, goodwife,' said Giles Musgrave; 'he shall be looked to as mine own son.'

'And what's that to a gentle lad that has always been tended as becomes him?'

'Heed not, mother! Be comforted! I must have gone to the wars, anyway. If so be I thrive, I'll send for thee to mine own castle, to reign there as I remember of old. Here now! Comfort Piers as thou only canst do.'

Piers, poor fellow, wept bitterly, only able to understand that something had befallen his comrade of seven years, which would take him away from field and moor. He clung to Hal, and both lads shed tears, till Hob roughly snatched Piers away and threw him to his aunt, with threats that drew indignant, though useless, interference from Hal, though Simon Bunce was muttering, 'As lief take one lad as the other!' while Dolly's angry defence of her nursling's wisdom broke the sadness of the parting.

CHAPTER XII. — A PRUDENT RECEPTION

```
So doth my heart misgive me in these conflicts,
  What may befall him to his harm and ours.
  —SHAKESPEARE.
```

Through the woods the party went to the fortified house of Threlkeld, where the gateway was evidently prepared to resist any passing attack, by stout gates and a little watch-tower.

Sir Giles blew a long blast on his bugle-horn, and had to repeat it twice before a porter looked cautiously out at a wicket opening in the heavy door, and demanded 'Who comes?'

'Open, porter, open in the name of King Harry, to the Lords of Clifford and of Peelholm.'

The porter fell back, observing, 'Sir, pardon, while I have speech with my master, Sir Lancelot Threlkeld.'

Some delay and some sounds of conversation were heard, then, on a renewed and impatient blast on Sir Giles's horn, Sir Lancelot Threlkeld himself came to the wicket, and his thin anxious voice might be heard demanding, 'What madness is this?'

'The madness is past, soundness is come,' responded Sir Giles. 'King Harry is on his throne, the traitors are fled, and your own fair son comes forth in his proper person to uphold the lawful sovereign; but he would fain first see his lady mother, and take her blessing with him.'

'And by his impatience destroy himself, after all the burthen of care and peril he hath been to me all these years,' lamented Sir Lancelot. 'But come in, fair lad. Open the gates, porter. I give you welcome, Lord Musgrave of Peelholm. But who are these?' he added, looking at the troop of buff-coated archers in the rear.

'They are bold champions of the Red Rose, returned Sir Giles, 'who have lived with me in the wolds, and now are on the way to maintain our King's quarrel.''

Sir Lancelot, however, would not hear of admitting the outlaws. Young Clifford and the Lord of Peelholm should be welcome, or more truly he could not help receiving them, but the archers must stay outside, their entertainment in beef and ale being committed to Bunce and the chief warder, while the two noblemen were conducted to the castle hall. For the first time in his life Clifford was received in his mother's home, and accepted openly, as he knelt before her to ask her blessing. A fine, active, handsome youth was he, with bright, keen eyes, close-curled black locks and hardy complexion, telling of his out-of-door life, and a free use of his limbs, and upright carriage, though still with more of the grace of the free mountain than of the training of pagedom and squiredom.

Nor could he speak openly and freely to her, not knowing how much he might say of his past intercourse with King Henry, and of her endeavour to discover it; and he sat beside her, neither of them greatly at ease, at the long table, which, by the array of silver cups, of glasses and the tall salt cellar separating the nobility and their followers, recalled to him dim recollections of the scenes of his youth.

He asked for his sister—he knew his little brother had died in the Netherlands—and he heard that she had been in the Priory of St. Helen's, and was now in the household of my Lady of Hungerford, who had promised to find a good match for her. There was but one son of the union with the knight of Threlkeld, and him Hal had never seen; nor was he at home, being a page in the household of the Earl of Westmoreland, according to the prevailing fashion of the castles of the great feudal nobles becoming schools of arms, courtesy and learning for the young gentlemen around. Indeed, Lady Clifford surveyed her eldest son with a sigh that such breeding was denied him, as she observed one or two little deficiencies in what would be called his table manners—not very important, but revealing that he had grown up in the byre instead of the castle, where there was a very strict and punctilious code, which figured in catechisms for the young.

She longed to keep him, and train him for his station, but in the first place, Sir Lancelot still held that it could not safely be permitted, since he had little confidence in the adherence of the House of Nevil to the Red Rose; and moreover Hal himself utterly refused to remain concealed in Cumberland instead of carrying his service to the King he loved.

In fact, when he heard the proposal of leaving him in the north, he stood up, and, with far more energy than had been expected from him, said, 'Go I must, to my lawful King's banner, and my father's cause. To King Harry I carry my homage and whatever my hand can do!'

Such an expression of energy lighted his hitherto dreamy eyes, that all beholders turned their glances on his face with a look of wonder. Sir Lancelot again objected that he would be rushing to his ruin.

'Be it so,' replied Hal. 'It is my duty.'

'The time seems to me to be come,' added Musgrave, 'that my young lord should put himself forward, though it may be only in a losing cause. Not so much for the sake of success, as to make himself a man and a noble.'

'But what can he do?' persisted Threlkeld; 'he has none of the training of a knight. How can you tilt in plate armour, you who have never bestridden a charger? These are not the days of Du Guesclin, when a lad came in from the byre and bore down all foes before him.'

The objection was of force, for the defensive armour of the fifteenth century had reached a pitch of cumbrousness that required long practice for a man to be capable of moving under it.

'So please you, sir,' said Hal, 'I am not wholly unskilled. The good Sir Giles and Simon Bunce have taught me enough to strike a blow with a good will for a good cause.'

'With horse and arms as befits him,' began Musgrave.

'I know not that a horse is here that could be depended on,' began Threlkeld. 'Armour too requires to be fitted and proved.'

He spoke in a hesitating voice that showed his unwillingness, and Hal exclaimed, 'My longbow is mine own, and so are my feet. Sir Giles, will you own me as an archer in your troop, where I will strive not to disgrace you or my name?'

'Bravely spoken, young lord,' said Sir Giles heartily; 'right willingly will I be your godfather in chivalry, since you find not one nigher home.'

'So may it best be,' observed his mother, 'since he is bent on going. Thus his name and rank may be kept back till it be plain whether the enmity of my Lords of Warwick and Montagu still remain against our poor house.'

There was no desire on either side to object when the Lord Musgrave of Peelholm decided on departing early on the morrow. Their host was evidently not sorry to speed them on their way, and his reluctant hospitality made them anxious to cumber him no longer than needful; and his mind was relieved when it was decided that the heir of the De Vescis and Cliffords should be known as Harry of Derwentdale.

Only, when all was preparation in the morning, and a hearty service had been said in the chapel, the lady called her son aside, and looking up into his dark eyes, said in a low voice, 'Be not angered with my lord husband's prudence, my son. Remember it is only by caution that he has saved thine head, or mine, or thy sister's!'

'Ay, ay, mother, I know,' he said, more impatiently than perhaps he knew.

'It was by the same care that he preserved us all when Edgecotefield was fought. Chafe not at him. Thou mayst be thankful even now, mayhap, to find a shelter preserved, while that rogue and robber Nevil holds our lands.'

'I am more like to have to protect thee, lady mother, and bring thee to thy true home again!' said Hal.

'Meantime, my child, take this purse and equip thyself at York or whenever thou canst. Nay, thou needst not shrug and refuse! How like thy father the gesture, though I would it were more gracious and seemly. But this is mine, mine own, none of my husband's, though he would be willing. It comes from the De Vesci lands, and those will be thine after me, and thine if thou winnest not back thy Clifford inheritance. And oh! my son, crave of Sir Giles to teach thee how to demean thyself that they may not say thou art but a churl.'

'I trust to be no churl in heart, if I be in manners,' said Hal, looking down on his small clinging mother.

'Only be cautious, my son. Remember that you are the last of the name, and it is your part to bring it to honour.'

'Which I shall scarce do by being cautious,' he said, with something of a smile. 'That was not my father's way.'

'Ah me! You have his spirit in you, and how did it end?'

'My Lord of Clifford,' said a voice from the court, 'you are waited for!'

'And remember,' cried his mother, with a last embrace, 'there will be safety here whenever thou shalt need it.'

'With God's grace, I am more like to protect you and your husband,' said the lad, bending for another kiss and hurrying away.

CHAPTER XIII. — FELLOW TRAVELLERS

```
And sickerlie she was of great disport,
  And full pleasant and amiable of port;
  Of small hounds had she that she fed
  With roasted flesh and milk and wastel bread.
  —CHAUCER.
```

Sir Giles Musgrave of Peelholm was an old campaigner, and when Hal came out beyond the gate of the Threlkeld fortalice, he found him reviewing his troop; a very disorderly collection, as Sir Lancelot pronounced with a sneer, looking out on them, and strongly advising his step-son not to cast in his lot with them, but to wait and see what would befall, and whether the Nevils were in earnest in their desertion of the House of York.

Hal restrained himself with difficulty enough to take a courteous leave of his mother's husband, to whose prudence and forbearance he was really much beholden; though, with his spirit newly raised and burning for his King, it was hard to have patience with neutrality.

He found Sir Giles employed in examining his followers, and rigidly sending home all not properly equipped with bow, sheaf of arrows, strong knife or pike, buff coat, head-piece and stout shoes; also a wallet of provisions for three days, or a certain amount of coin. He would have no marauding on the way, and refused to take any mere lawless camp follower, thus disposing of a good many disreputable-looking fellows who had flocked in his wake. Sir Lancelot's steward seconded him heartily by hunting back his master's retainers; and there remained only about five-and-twenty—mostly, in fact, yeomen or their sons—men who had been in arms for Queen Margaret and had never made their submission, but lived on unmolested in the hills, really outlawed, but not coming in collision with the authorities enough to have their condition inquired into. They had sometimes attacked Yorkist parties, sometimes resisted Scottish raids, or even made a foray in return, and they were well used to arms. These all had full equipments, and some more coin in their pouches than they cared to avow. Three or four of them brought an ox, calf or sheep, or a rough pony loaded with provisions, and driven by a herd boy or a son eager to see life and 'the wars.' Simon Bunce, well armed, was of this party. Hob Hogward, though he had come to see what became of his young lord, was pronounced too stiff and aged to join the band, which might now really be called a troop, not a mere lawless crowd of rough lads. There were three trained men-at-arms, the regular retainers of Sir Giles, who held a little peel tower on the borders where nobody durst molest him, and these marshalled the little band in fair order.

It was no season for roses, but a feather was also the cognisance of Henry VI., and every one's barret-cap mounted a feather, generally borrowed from the goodwife's poultry yard at home, but sometimes picked up on the moors, and showing the barred black and brown patterns of the hawk's or the owl's plumage. It was a heron's feather that Hal assumed, on the counsel of Sir Giles, who told him it was an old badge of the Cliffords, and it became well his bright dark hair and brown face.

On they went, a new and wonderful march to Hal, who had only looked with infant eyes on anything beyond the fells, and had very rarely been into a little moorland church, or seen enough people together for a market day in Penrith. Sir Giles directed their course along the sides of the hills till he should gain further intelligence, and know how they would be received. For the most part the people were well inclined to King Henry, though unwilling to stir on his behalf in fear of Edward's cruelty.

However, it was as they had come down from the hills intending to obtain fresh provisions at one of the villages, and Hal was beginning to recognise the moors he had known in earlier childhood, that they perceived a party on the old Roman road before them, which the outlaws' keen eyes at once discovered to be somewhat of their own imputed trade. There seemed to be a waggon upset, persons bound, and a buzz of men, like wasps around a honeycomb preying on it. Something like women's veiled forms could be seen. 'Ha! Mere robbery. This must not be. Upon them! Form! Charge!' were the brief commands of the leader, and the compact body ran at a rapid but a regulated pace down the little slope that gave them an advantage of ground with some concealment by a brake of gorse. 'Halt! Pikes forward!' was the next order. The little band were already close upon the robbers, in whom they began to recognise some of those whom Sir Giles had dismissed as mere ruffians unequipped a few days before. It was with a yell of indignation that the troop fell on them, Sir Giles with a sharp blow severing the bridle of a horse that a man was leading, but there was a cry back, 'We are for King Harry! These be Yorkists!'

'Nay! nay!' came back the voices of the overthrown. 'Help! help! for King Harry and Queen Margaret! These be rank thieves who have set on us! Holy women are here!'

These exclamations came broken and in utter confusion, mingled with cries for mercy and asseverations on the part of the thieves, and fierce shouts from Sir Giles's men. All was hubbub, barking dogs, shouting men, and Hal scarcely knew anything till he was aware of two or three shrouded nuns, as it seemed, standing by their ponies, of merchantmen or carters trying to quiet and harness frightened mules, of waggons overturned, of a general confusion over which arose Lord Musgrave's powerful authoritative voice.

'Kit of Clumber! Why should I not hang you for thieving on yonder tree, with your fellow thieves?'

'Yorkists, sir! It was all in the good cause,' responded a sullen voice, as a grim red and scarred face was seen on a ruffian held by two of the archers.

'No Yorkists we, sir!' began a stout figure, coming forward from the waggon. 'We be peaceable merchants and this is a holy dame, the—'

'The Prioress Selby of Greystone,' interrupted one of the nuns, coming forward with a hawk on her wrist. 'Sir Giles of Musgrave, I am beholden to you! I was on my way to take the young damsel of Bletso to her father, the Lord St. John, with Earl Warwick in London. He sent us an escort, but they being arrant cravens, as it seems, we thought it well to join company with these same merchants, and thus we became a bait for the outlaws of the Border.'

'Lady, lady,' burst from one of the prisoners, 'I swear that we kenned not holy dames to be of the company! Sir, my lord, we thought to serve the cause of King Harry, and how any man is to guess which side is Earl Warwick's is past an honest man.'

'An honest man whose cause is his own pouch!' returned Sir Giles. 'Miscreants all! But I trow we are scarce yet out of the land of misrule! So if the Lady Prioress will say a word for such a sort of sorners, I'll e'en let you go on your way.'

'They have had a warning, the poor rogues, and that will suffice for this time! Nay, now, fellows, let my wimple alone! You'll not find another lord to let you off so easy, nor another Prioress to stand your friend. Get off, I say.'

An archer enforced her words with a blow, and by some means, rough or otherwise, a certain amount of order was restored, the ruffians slinking off among the gorse bushes, their flight hastened by the pointing of pikes and levelling of arrows at them. While the merchants, diving into their packages, produced horns of ale which a younger man offered to their defenders, the chief of the party, a portly fellow, interrupted certain civilities between the Prioress and Sir Giles by praying them to partake of a cup of malmsey, and adding an entreaty that they might be allowed to join company with so brave an escort, explaining that he was a poor merchant of London and the Hans towns who had been beguiled into an expedition to Scotland to the young King James, who was said to have a fair taste. He waved his hands as if his sufferings had been beyond description.

'Went for wool and came back shorn!' said the Prioress, laughing. 'Well, my Lord Musgrave, what say you to letting us join company?—as I see your band is afoot it will be no great delay, and the more the safer as well as the merrier! Here, let me present to you my young maid, the Lady Anne of Bletso, whom I in person am about to deliver to her father.'

'And let me present privately to both ladies,' said Sir Giles, 'the young squire Harry of Derwentdale, who hath been living as a shepherd in the hills during the York rule.'

'Ha! my lord, methinks this may not be the first meeting between Lady Anne and you, though she would not know who the herd boy was who found her, a stray lambkin on the moor.'

The young people looked at each other with eyes of recognition, and as Hal made his best bow, he said, 'Forsooth, lady, I did not know myself till afterwards.'

'Your shepherd and his wife gave me to understand that I should do hurt by inquiring too much,' said the young lady smiling, and holding out her hand, which Hal did not know whether to kiss or to shake. 'I hope the kind old goodwife is well, who cosseted me so lovingly.'

'She fares well, indeed, lady, only grieved at parting with me.'

'There now,' said the Prioress, 'since we are quit of the robbers, methinks we cannot do better than halt awhile for Master Lorimer's folk to mend the tackling of their gear, while we make our noonday meal and provide for our further journey. Allow me to be your hostess for the nonce, my lords.'

And between the lady's sumpter mules and the merchant's stores a far more sumptuous meal was produced than would have otherwise been the share of the Lancastrian party.

CHAPTER XIV. — THE JOURNEY

'Twas sweet to see these holy maids,
   Like birds escaped to greenwood shades,
—SCOTT.

The Prioress Agnes Selby of Greystone was a person who would have made a much fitter lady of a castle than head of a nunnery. She would have worked for and with her lord, defended his lands for him, governed his house and managed her sons with untiring zest and energy. But a vow of her parents had consigned her to a monastic life at York, where she could only work off her vigour by teasing the more devout and grave sisters, and when honourably banished to the more remote Greystone, in field sports, and in fortifying her convent against Scots or Lancastrians who, somewhat to her disappointment, never did attack her. No complaint or scandal had ever attached itself to her name, and she let Mother Scholastica manage the nuns, and regulate the devotions, while Greystone was known as a place where a thirsty warrior might be refreshed, where tales and ballads of Border raids were welcome, and where good hawk or hound was not despised.

It had occurred to the Lord St. John of Bletso that the little daughter whom he had left at York might be come to a marriageable age, and he had listened to the proposal of one of the cousins of the house of Nevil for a contract between her and his son, sending an escort northwards to fetch her, properly accompanied.

She had been all these years at Greystone, and the Prioress immediately decided that this would be an excellent opportunity of seeing the southern world, and going on a round of pilgrimages which would make the expedition highly decorous. The ever restless spirit within her rose in delight, and the Sisterhood of York were ready to acquiesce, having faith in Mother Agnes' good sense to guide her and her pupil to his castle in Bedfordshire by the help of Father Martin through any tangles of the White and Red Roses that might await her, as well to her real principle for avoiding actual evil, though she might startle monastic proprieties.

There was no doubt but that conversation, when she could have it, was as great a joy to her as ever was galloping after a deer; and there she sat with her beautiful hound by her side, and her hawk on a pole, exchanging sentiments of speculation as to Warwick's change of front with Sir Giles Musgrave, Father Martin, and Master Ralph Lorimer, while discussing a pasty certainly very superior to anything that had come out of the Penrith stores.

Young Clifford and Lady Anne sat on the grass near, too shy for the present to renew their acquaintance, but looking up at one another under their eyelashes, and the first time their eyes met, the girl breaking into a laugh, but it was not till towards the end of the refection that they were startled into intercourse by a general growling and leaping up of the great hound, and of the two big ungainly dogs chained to the waggon, as wet, lean, bristling but ecstatic, Watch dashed in among them, and fell on his master.

For four days (unless he was tied up at first) the good dog must have been tracking him. 'Off! off!' cried the Prioress, holding back her deer-hound by main strength. 'Off, Florimond! he sets thee a pattern of faithfulness! Be quiet and learn thy devoir!'

'O sir, I cannot send him back!' entreated Hal, also embracing and caressing the shaggy neck.

'Send him back! Nay, indeed. As saith the Reverend Mother, it were well if some earls and lords minded his example,' said Sir Giles.

'Here! Watch, I mind thee well,' added Anne. 'Here's a slice of pasty to reward thee. Oh! thou art very hungry,' as the big mouth bolted it whole.

'Nearly famished, poor rogue!' said Hal, administering a bone. 'How far hast thou run, mine own lad! Art fain to come with thy master and see the hermit?'

'Thou must e'en go,' growled Simon Bunce, 'unless the lady's dog make an end of thee! 'Tis ever the worthless that turn up.'

'I would Florimond would show himself as true,' said the Prioress. 'Don't show thy teeth, sir! I can honour Watch, yet love thee.'

''Tis jealousy as upsets faith,' said the merchant. 'The hound is a knightly beast with his proud head, but he brooks not to see a Woodville creep in.'

'Nay, or a Beaufort!' suggested Sir Giles.

'No treason, Lord Musgrave!' said the Prioress, laughing.

'Ah, madam,' responded Sir Giles, 'what is treason?'

'Whatever is against him that has the best of it,' observed Master Lorimer. 'Well that it is not the business of a poor dealer in horse-gear and leather- work. He asks not which way his bridles are to turn! How now, Tray and Blackchaps? Never growl and gird. You have no part in the fray!'

For they were chained, and could only champ, bark and howl, while Florimond and Watch turned one another over, and had to be pulled forcibly back, by Hal on the one hand and on the other by the Mother Agnes, who would let nobody touch Florimond except herself. After this, the two dogs subsided into armed neutrality, and gradually became devoted friends.

The curiously composed cavalcade moved on their way southward. The Prioress was mounted on the fine chestnut horse that Sir Giles had rescued. She was attended by a nun, Sister Mabel, and a lay Sister, both as hardy as herself, and riding sturdy mountain ponies; but her chaplain, a thin delicate-looking man with a bad cough, only ventured upon a sturdy ass; Anne St. John had a pretty little white palfrey and two men-at-arms. There were two grooms, countrymen, who had run away on the onset of the thieves, but came sneaking back again, to be soundly rated by the Prioress, who threatened to send them home again or have them well scourged, but finally laughed and forgave them.

The merchant, Master Lorimer—who dealt primarily in all sorts of horse furniture, but added thereto leather-work for knights and men-at-arms, and all that did not too closely touch the armourer's trade—had three sturdy attendants, having lost one in an attack by the Scottish Borderers, and he had four huge Flemish horses, who sped along the better for their loads having been lightened by sales in Edinburgh, where he had hardly obtained skins enough to make up for the weight. His headquarters, he said, were at Barnet, since tanning and leather-dressing, necessary to his work, though a separate guild, literally stank in the nostrils of the citizens of London.

To these were added Sir Giles Musgrave's twenty archers, making a very fair troop, wherewith to proceed, and the Prioress decided on not going to York. She was not particularly anxious for an interview with the Abbess of her Order, and it would have considerably lengthened the journey, which both Musgrave and Lorimer were anxious to make as short as possible. They preferred likewise to keep to the country, that was still chiefly open and wild, with all its destiny in manufactories yet to come, though there were occasionally such towns, villages and convents on the way where provisions and lodging could be obtained.

Every fresh scene of civilisation was a new wonder to Hal Clifford, and scarcely less so to Anne St. John, though her life in the moorland convent had begun when she was not quite so young as he had been when taken to the hills of Londesborough. He had only been two or three times in the church at Threlkeld, which was simple and bare, and the full display of a monastic church was an absolute amazement, making him kneel almost breathless with awe, recollecting what the royal hermit had told him. He was too illiterate to follow the service, but the music and the majestic flow of the chants overwhelmed him, and he listened with hands clasped over his face, not daring to raise his eyes to the dazzling gold of the altar, lighted by innumerable wax tapers.

The Prioress was amused. 'Art dazed, my friend? This is but a poor country cell; we will show you something much finer when we get to Derby.'

Hal drew a long breath. 'Is that meant to be like the saints in Heaven?' he said. 'Is that the way they sing there?'

'I should hope they pronounce their Latin better,' responded the Prioress, who, it may be feared, was rather a light-minded woman. At any rate there was a chill upon Hal which prevented him from directing any of his remarks or questions to her for the future. The chaplain told him something of what he wanted to know, but he met with the most sympathy from the Lady Anne.

'Which, think you, is the fittest temple and worship?' he said; as they rode out together, after hearing an early morning service, gone through in haste, and partaking of a hurried meal. The sun was rising over the hills of Derbyshire, dyeing them of a red purple, standing out sharply against a flaming sky, flecked here and there with rosy clouds, and fading into blue that deepened as it rose higher. The elms and beeches that bordered the monastic fields had begun to put on their autumn livery, and yellow leaves here and there were like sparks caught from the golden light.

Hal drew off his cap as in homage to the glorious sight.

'Ah, it is fine!' said Anne, 'it is like the sunrise upon our own moors, when one breathes freely, and the clouds grow white instead of grey.'

'Ah!' said Hal, 'I used to go out to the high ground and say the prayer the hermit taught me—"Jam Lucis," it began. He said it was about the morning light.'

'I know that "Jam Lucis,"' said Anne; 'the Sisters sing it at prime, and Sister Scholastica makes us think how it means about light coming and our being kept from ill,' and she hummed the chant of the first verse.

'I think this blue sky and royal sun, and the moon and stars at night, are God's great hall of praise,' said Hal, still keeping his cap off, as he had done through Anne's chant of praise.

'Verily it is! It is the temple of God Almighty, Creator of Heaven and earth, as the Credo says,' replied Anne, 'but, maybe, we come nearer still to Him in God the Son when we are in church.'

'I do not know. The dark vaulted roof and the dimness seem to crush me down,' said the mountain lad, 'though the singing lifts me sometimes, though at others it comes like a wailing gust, all mournful and sad! If I could only understand! My royal hermit would tell me when I can come to him.'

'Do you think, now he is a king again, he will be able to take heed to you?'

'I know he cares for me,' said Hal with confidence.

'Ah yea, but will the folk about him care to let him talk to you? I have heard say that he was but a puppet in their hands. Yea, you are a great lord, that is true, but will that great masterful Earl Warwick let you to him, or say all these thoughts of his and yours are but fancies for babes?'

'Simon Bunce did mutter such things, and that one of us was as great an innocent as the other,' said Hal, 'but I trust my hermit's love.'

'Ay, you know you are going to someone you love, and who loves you,' sighed Anne, 'but how will it be with me?'

'Your father?' suggested Hal.

'My father! What knows he of me or I of him? I tell thee, Harry Clifford, he left me at York when I was not eight years old, and I have never seen him since. He gave a charge on his lands to a goldsmith at York to pay for my up- bringing, and I verily believe thought no more of me than if I had been a messan dog. He wedded a lady in Flanders and had a son or twain, but I have never seen them nor my stepdame; and now Gilbert there, who brought the letter to the Mother Prioress, says she is dead, and the little heir, whose birth makes me nobody, is at a monastery school at Ghent. But my Lord of Redgrave must needs make overtures to my father for me, whether for his son or himself Gilbert cannot say. So my father sends to bring me back for a betrothal. The good Prioress goes with me. She saith that if it be the old Lord, who is a fierce old rogue with as ill a name as Tiptoft himself, the butcher, she will make my Lord St. John know the reason why! But what will he care?'

'It would be hard not to hear my Lady Prioress!' said Hal, looking back at the determined black figure, gesticulating as she talked to Sir Giles.

Anne laughed, half sadly, 'So you think! But you have never seen the grim faces at Bletso! They will say she is but a woman and a nun, and what are her words to alliance with a friend of the Lord of Warwick? Ah! it is a heartless hope, when I come to that castle!'

'Nay, Anne, if my King gives me my place then&&

'Lady Anne! Lady Anne!' called Sir Giles Musgrave, 'the Mother Prioress thinks it not safe for you to keep so much in the front. There might be ill- doers in the thickets.'

Anne perforce reined in, but Hal fed on the idea that had suddenly flashed on him.

CHAPTER XV. — BLETSO

Matter of marriage was the charge he gave me.
  —SHAKESPEARE,

The cavalcade journeyed on not very quickly, as the riders accommodated themselves to those on foot. They avoided the towns when they came into the more inhabited country, the Prioress preferring the smaller hostels for pilgrims and travellers, and, it may be suspected, monasteries to the nunneries, where she said the ladies had nothing to talk about but wonder at her journey, and advice to stay in shelter till after the winter weather. Meantime it was a fine autumn still, and with bright colours on the woods, where deer, hare, rabbit, or partridge tempted the hounds, not to say their mistress, but she kept them well in leash, and her falcon with hood and jesses, she being too well nurtured not to be well aware of the strict laws of the chase, except when some good-natured monk gave her leave and accompanied her—generally Augustinians, who were more of country squires than ecclesiastics. Watch needed no leash—he kept close to his master, except when occasionally tempted to a little amateur shepherding, from which Hal could easily call him off. The great stag-hounds evidently despised him, and the curs of the waggon hated him, and snarled whenever he came near them, but the Prioress respected him, and could well believe that the hermit King had loved him. 'He had just the virtues to suit the good King Harry,' she said, 'dutifulness and harmlessness.'

The Prioress was the life of the party, with her droll descriptions of the ways of the nuns who received her, while the males of the party had to be content with the hostel outside. Sir Giles and Master Lorimer, riding on each side of her, might often be heard laughing with her. The young people were much graver, especially as there were fewer and fewer days' journeys to Bletso, and Anne's unknown future would begin with separation from all she had ever known, unless the Mother Prioress should be able to remain with her.

And to Harry Clifford the loss of her presence grew more and more to be dreaded as each day's companionship drew them nearer together in sympathy, and he began to build fanciful hopes of the King's influence upon the plans of Lord St. John, unless the contract of betrothal had been actually made, and therewith came a certain zest in looking to his probable dignity such as he had never felt before.

The last day's journey had come. The escort who had acted as guides were in familiar fields and lanes, and one, the leader, rode up to Lady Anne and pointed to the grey outline among the trees of her home, while he sent the other to hurry forward and announce her.

Anne shivered a little, and Hal kept close to her. He had made the journey on foot, because he had chosen to be reckoned among Musgrave's archers till he had received full knightly training; and, besides, he had more freedom to attach himself to Anne's bridle rein, and be at hand to help through difficult passages. Now he came up close to her, and she held out her hand. He pressed it warmly.

'You will not forget?'

'Never, never! That red rose in the snow—I have the leaf in my breviary. And Goodwife Dolly, tell her I'll never forget how she cosseted the wildered lamb.'

'Poor Mother Dolly, when shall I see her?'

'Oh! you will be able to have her to share your state, and Watch too! I take none with me.'

'If we are all in King Harry's cause, there will be hope of meeting, and then if—'

'Ah! I see a horseman coming! Is it my father?'

It was a horseman who met them, taking off his cap of maintenance and bowing low to the Prioress and the young lady, but it was the seneschal of the castle, not the father whom Anne so dreaded, but an old gentleman, Walter Wenlock, with whom there was a greeting as of an old friend. My lord had gone with the Earl of Warwick to Queen Margaret in France, and had sent a messenger with a letter to meet his daughter at York, and tell her to go to the house of the Poor Clares in London instead of coming home, 'and there await him.'

The route that had been taken by the party accounted for their not having met the messenger and it was plain that they must go on to London. The evening was beginning to draw in, and a night's lodging was necessary. Anne assumed a little dignity.

'My good friends who have guarded me, I hope you will do me the honour to rest for the night in my father's castle.'

The seneschal bowed acquiescence, but the poor man was evidently sorely perplexed by such an extensive invitation on the part of his young lady on his peace establishment, though the Prioress did her best to assist Anne to set him at ease. 'Here is Sir Giles Musgrave, the Lord of Peelholm on the Borders, a staunch friend of King Harry, with a band of stout archers, and this gentleman from the north is with him.' (It had been agreed that the Clifford name should not be mentioned till the way had been felt with Warwick, one of whose cousins had been granted the lands of the Black Lord Clifford.)

The seneschal bent before Musgrave courteously, saying he was happy to welcome so good and brave a knight, and he prayed his followers to excuse if their fare was scant and homely, being that he was unprovided for the honour.

'No matter, sir,' returned Musgrave; 'we are used to soldiers' fare.'

'And,' proceeded Anne, 'Master Lorimer must lie here, and his wains.'

'Master Lorimer,' said the Prioress, 'with whom belike—Lorimer of Barnet —Sir Seneschal has had dealings,' and she put forward the merchant, who had been falling back to his waggon.

'Yea,' said Walter Wenlock frankly, holding out his hand. 'We have bought your wares and made proof of them, good sir. I am glad to welcome you, though I never saw you to the face before.'

'Great thanks, good seneschal. All that I would ask would be licence for my wains to stand in your court to-night while my fellows and I sup and lodge at the hostel.'

The hospitality of Bletso could not suffer this, and both Anne and the seneschal were urgent that all should remain, Wenlock reflecting that if the store for winter consumption were devoured, even to the hog waiting to be killed, he could obtain fresh supplies from the tenants, so he ushered all into the court, and summoned steward, cooks, and scullions to do their best. It was not a castle, only a castellated house, which would not have been capable of long resistance in time of danger, but the court and stables gave ample accommodation for the animals and the waggons, and the men were bestowed in the great open hall, reaching to the top of the house, where all would presently sup.

In the meantime the seneschal conducted the ladies and their two attendants to a tiny chamber, where an enormous bed was being made ready by the steward's wife and her son, and in which all four ladies would sleep, the Prioress and Anne one way, the other two foot to foot with them! They had done so before, so were not surprised, and the lack of furniture was a matter of course. Their mails were brought up, a pitcher of water and a bowl, and they made their preparations for supper. Anne was in high spirits at the dreaded meeting, and still more dreaded parting, having been deferred, and she skipped about the room, trying to gather up her old recollections. 'Yes, I remember that bit of tapestry, and the man that stands there among the sheep. Is it King David, think you, Mother, about to throw his stone at the lion and the bear?'

'Lion and bear, child! 'Tis the three goddesses and Paris choosing the fairest to give the golden apple.'

'Methought that was the lion's mane, but I see a face.'

'What would the Lady Venus say to have her golden locks taken for a lion's mane?'

'I like black hair,' said Anne.

'Better not fix thy mind on any hue! We poor women have no choice save what fathers make for us.'

'O good my mother, peace! They are all in France, and there's no need to spoil this breathing time with thinking of what is coming! Good old Wenlock! I used to ride on his shoulder! I'm right glad to see him again! I must tell him in his ear to put Hal well above the salt! May not I tell him in his ear who he is?'

'Safer not, my maid, till we know what King Harry can do for him. Better that his name should not get abroad till he can have his own.'

A great bell brought all down, and Anne was pleased to see that her seneschal made no question about placing Harry Clifford beside the Prioress, who sat next to the Lord of Peelholm, who sat next to the young daughter of the house in the seat of honour.

The nuns, Master Lorimer, and one of the archers, who was a Border squire, besides Master Wenlock, occupied the high table on the dais, and the archers, grooms, and the rest of the houschold were below.

The fare was not scanty nor unsubstantial, but evidently hastily prepared, being chiefly broiled slices of beef, on which salting had begun; but there was a lack of bread, even of barley, though there was no want of drink.

However, the Prioress was good-humoured, and forestalled all excuses by jests about travellers' meals and surprises in the way of guests, and both she and Sir Giles were anxious for Wenlock's news of the state of things.

He knew much more of the course of affairs than they in their northern homes and on their journey.

'The realm is divided,' he said. 'Those who hold to King Harry, as you gentles do, are in high joy, but there be many, spoken with respect, who cannot face about so fast, and hold still for York, though they mislike the Queen's kindred. Of such are the merchantmen of London.'

'Is it so?' asked Lorimer. 'If King Edward be as deep in debt to them as to me for housings and bridle reins methinks he should not be in good odour in their nostrils.'

'Yea,' said Wenlock, 'but if he be gone a beggar to Burgundy what becomes of their debt?'

'I would not give much for it were he restored a score of times,' said the Prioress. 'What would he do but plunge deeper?'

'There would be hope, though, of getting an order on the royal demesne, or the crown jewels, or the taxes,' said Lorimer. 'Nay, I hold one even now that will be but waste if he come not back.'

'And this poor King spendeth nothing save on priests and masses,' said Wenlock.

Hal started forward, eager to hear of his King, and Musgrave said, 'A holy man is he.'

'Too holy for a King,' said the seneschal. 'He looked like a woolsack across a horse when my Lord of Warwick led him down Cheapside; and only the rabble cried out "Long live King Harry!" but some scoffed and said they saw a mere gross monk with a baby face where they had been wont to see a comely prince full of manhood, with a sword instead of beads.'

'His son will please them,' said Musgrave. 'He was a goodly child, full of spirit, when last I saw him.'

'If so be he have not too much of the Frenchwoman, his mother, in him,' said Wenlock. 'A losing lot, as poor as any rats, and as proud as very peacocks.'

'She was gracious enough and won all hearts on the Border,' replied Musgrave.

'Come, come!' put in the Prioress, 'you may have the chance yet to break a lance on her behalf. No fear but she is royal enough to shine down King Edward's low-born love, the Widow Grey!'

'Ay, there lay the cause of discontent,' said Lorimer; 'the upstart ways of her kin were not to be borne. To hear Dick Woodville chaffer about the blazoning of his horse-gear when he was wedding the fourscore-year-old Duchess of Norfolk, one would have thought he was an emperor at the very least.'

'Widow Grey has done something for her husband's cause,' said the seneschal, 'in bringing him at last a fair son, all in his exile, and she in sanctuary at Westminster. The London citizens are ever touched through all the fat about their hearts by whatever would sound well in the mouth of a ballad-monger.'

'My King, my King, what of him?' sighed Hal in the Prioress's ear, and she made the inquiry for him: 'What said you of King Henry, Sir Seneschal? How did he fare in his captivity?'

'Not so ill, methinks,' said the seneschal. 'He had the range of the Tower, and St. Peter's in the Fetters to pray in, which was what he heeded most; also he had a messan dog, and a tame bird. Indeed, men said he had laid on much flesh since he had been mewed up there; and my lord, who went with my Lord of Warwick to fetch him, said his garments were scarce so cleanly as befitted. 'Twas hard to make him understand. First he clasped his hands, and bowed his head, crying out that he forgave those who came to slay him, and when he found it was all the other way, he stood like one dazed, let his hand be kissed, and they say is still in the hands of my Lord Archbishop of York just as if he were the waxen image of St. John in a procession.'

'The Earl and the Queen will have to do the work,' said the Prioress, 'and they will no more hold together than a couple of wild hawks will hunt in company. How long do you give them to tear out one another's eyes?'

'Son and daughter may keep them together,' said Musgrave,

'Hatred of the Woodvilles is more like, a poor band though it be,' said the Prioress. 'These are stirring times! I'll not go back to my anchoress lodge in the north till I see what works out of them! Meantime, to our beds, sweet Anne, since 'tis an early start tomorrow.'

The Prioress, who had become warmly interested in Hal, and had divined the feeling between him and Anne, thought that if she could obtain access to the Archbishop of York, Warwick's brother George, she could deal with him to procure Clifford's restitution in name and in blood, and at least his De Vesci inheritance, if Dick Nevil, who had grasped the Clifford lands, could not be induced to give them up.

'I have seen George Nevil,' she said, 'when I was instituted to Greystone. He is of kindlier mood than his brothers, and more a valiant trencherman and hunter than aught else. If I had him on the moors and could show him some sport with a red deer, I could turn him round my finger.'

CHAPTER XVI. — THE HERMIT IN THE TOWER

Thy pity hath been balm to heal their wounds,
  Thy mildness hath allayed their swelling griefs,
  Thy mercy dried their ever flowing tears.
  —SHAKESPEARE.

Early in the morning, while the wintry sun was struggling with mists, and grass and leaves were dark with frost, the Prioress was in her saddle. Perhaps the weather might have constrained a longer stay, but that it was clear to her keen eyes that, however welcome Wenlock might make his young lady, there was little provision and no welcome for thorough-going Lancastrians like Sir Giles's troop, who had besides a doubtful Robin Hood-like reputation; and as neither she nor Anne wished to ride forward without them, they decided to go on all together as before.

And a very wet and slightly snowy journey they had, 'meeting in snow and parting in snow,' as Hal said, as he marched by Anne's bridle-rein, leading her pony, so as to leave her hands free to hold cloak and hood close about her.

She sighed, and put one hand on his, but a gust of wind took that opportunity of getting under her cloak and sending it fluttering over her back, so that he had to catch it and return it to her grasp.

'Let us take that as a prophecy that storms shall not hinder our further meeting! It may be! It may be! Who knows what my King may do for us?'

'Only a storm can bring us together! But that may—'

Her breath was blown away again before the sentence was finished, if it was meant to be finished, and Master Lorimer came to insist on the ladies taking shelter in his covered waggon, where the Prioress was already installed.

Through rain and sleet they reached Chipping Barnet in due time on the third day's journey, and here they were to part from the merchant's wains. He had sent forward, and ample cheer was provided at the handsome timbered and gabled house at the porch of which stood his portly wife, with son, daughter, and son-in-law, ready to welcome the party, bringing them in to be warmed and dried before sitting down to the excellent meal which it had been Mistress Lorimer's pride and pleasure to provide. There was a small nunnery at Barnet, but not very near, and the Prioress Agnes did not think herself bound to make her way thither in the dark and snow, so she remained, most devoutly waited on by her hostess, and discussed the very last tidings, which had been brought that morning by the foreman whom Mistress Lorimer had sent to bring the news to her husband.

It was probable that the Lord of Bletso was with Warwick and the Queen, as he had not been heard of at his home. The King was in the royal apartments of the Tower, under the charge of the Chancellor. The Earl of Oxford, a steady partisan of the Red Rose, was Constable of the Kingdom, and was guarding the Tower.

On hearing this, Musgrave decided to repair at once to the Earl, one of the few men in whom there was confidence, since he had never changed his allegiance, and to take his counsel as to the recognition of young Clifford. On the way to the Tower they would leave the Prioress and her suite at the Sister Minoresses', till news could be heard of the Baron St. John.

So for the last time the travellers rode forth in slightly improved weather. Harry's heart beat high with the longing soon to be in the presence of him who had opened so many doors of life to his young mind, whom he so heartily loved, and who, it might be, could give him that which he began to feel would be the joy of his life.

The archers, who had been lodged in the warehouses, were drawn up in a compact body, and Master Lorimer, who had a shop in Cheapside, decided on accompanying them, partly to be at the scene of action and partly to facilitate their entrance.

So Hal walked by the side of Anne St. John's bridle-rein, with a very full heart, swelling with sensations he did not understand, and which kept him absolutely silent, untrained as he was in the conventionalities which would have made speech easier to him. Nor had Anne much more command of tongue, and all she did was to keep her hand upon the shoulder of her squire; but there was much involuntary meaning in the yearning grasp of those fingers, and both fed on the hopes the Prioress had given them.

Christmas was close at hand, and fatted cattle on their way to market impeded the way, so that Hal's time was a good deal taken up in steering the pony along, and in preventing Watch from getting into a battle with the savage dogs that guarded them. Penrith market, where once he had been, had never shown him anything like such a concourse, and he could hear muttered exclamations from the archers, who walked by Sir Giles's orders in a double line on each side the horses, their pikes keeping off the blundering approach of bullocks or sheep. 'By the halidome, if the Scots were among them, they might victual their whole kingdom till Domesday!'

The tall spire of old St. Paul's and the four turrets of the Tower began to rise on them, and were pointed out by Master Lorimer, for even Sir Giles had only once in his life visited the City, and no one else of the whole band from the north had ever been there. The road was bordered by the high walls of monasteries, overshadowed by trees, and at the deep gateway of one of these Lorimer called a halt. It was the house of the Minoresses or Poor Clares, where the ladies were to remain. The six weeks' companionship would come to an end, and the Prioress was heartily sorry for it. 'I shall scarce meet such good company at the Clares',' she said, laughing, as she took leave of Lord Musgrave, 'Mayhap when I go back to my hills I shall remember your goodwife's offer of hospitality, Master Lorimer.'

Master Lorimer bowed low, expressed his delight in the prospect, and kissed the Prioress's hand, but the heavy door was already being opened, and with an expressive look of drollery and resignation, the good lady withdrew her hand, hastily brought her Benedictine hood and veil closely over her face, and rode into the court, followed by her suite. Anne had time to let her hand be kissed by Sir Giles and Hal, who felt as if a world had closed on him as the heavy doors clanged together behind the Sisters. But the previous affection of his young life lay before him as Sir Giles rode on to the fortified Aldgate, and after a challenge from the guard, answered by a watchword from Lorimer, and an inquiry for whom the knight held, they were admitted, and went on through an increasing crowd trailing boughs of holly and mistletoe, to the north gateway of the Tower. Here they parted with Lorimer, with friendly greetings and promises to come and see his stall at Cheapside.

There was a man-at-arms with the star of the De Veres emblazoned on his breast, and a red rosette on his steel cap, but he would not admit the new-comers till Sir Giles had given his name, and it had been sent in by another of the garrison to the Earl of Oxford.

Presently, after some waiting in the rain, and looking up with awe at the massive defences, two knights appeared with outstretched hands of welcome. Down went the drawbridge, up went the portcullis, the horses clattered over the moat, and the reception was hearty indeed. 'Well met, my Lord of Musgrave! I knew you would soon be where Red Roses grew.'

'Welcome, Sir Giles! Methought you had escaped after the fight at Hexham.'

'Glad indeed to meet you, brave Sir John, and you, good Lord of Holmdale! Is all well with the King?'

'As well as ever it will be. The Constable is nigh at hand! You have brought us a stout band of archers, I see! We will find a use for them if March chooses to show his presumptuous nose here again!'

'And hither comes my Lord Constable! It rejoices his heart to hear of such staunch following.'

The Earl of Oxford, a stern, grave man of early middle age, was coming across the court-yard, and received Sir Giles with the heartiness that became the welcome of a proved and trustworthy ally. After a few words, Musgrave turned and beckoned to Hal, who advanced, shy and colouring.

'Ha! young Lord Clifford! I am glad to see you! I knew your father well, rest his soul! The King spoke to me of the son of a loyal house living among the moors.'

'The King was very good to me,' faltered Hal, crimson with eagerness.

'Ay, ay! I sent not after you, having enough to do here; and besides, till we have the strong hand, and can do without that heady kinsman of Warwick, it will be ill for you to disturb the rogue—what's his name—to whom your lands have been granted, and who might turn against the cause and maybe make a speedy end of you if he knew you present. Be known for the present as Sir Giles counsels. Better not put his name forward,' he added to Musgrave.

'I care not for lands,' said Hal, 'only to see the King.'

'See him you shall, my young lord, and if he be not in one of his trances, he will be right glad to see you and remember you. But he is scarce half a man,' added Oxford, turning to Musgrave. 'Cares for nought but his prayers! Keeps his Hours like a monk! We can hardly bring him to sit in the Council, and when he is there he sits scarce knowing what we say. 'Tis my belief, when the Queen and Prince come, that we shall have to make the Prince rule in his name, and let him alone to his prayers! He will be in the church. 'Tis nones, or some hour as they call it, and he makes one stretch out to another.'

They entered the low archway of St. Peter ad Vincula, and there Hal perceived a figure in a dark mantle just touched with gold, kneeling near the chancel step, almost crouching. Did he not know the attitude, though the back was broader than of old? He paused, as did his companions; but there was one who did not pause, and would not be left outside. Watch unseen had pattered up, and was rearing up, jumping and fawning. There was a call of 'Watch! here sirrah!' but 'Watch! Watch! Good dog! Is it thou indeed?' was exclaimed at the same moment, and with Watch springing up, King Henry stood on his feet looking round with his dazed glance.

'My King! my hermit father! Forgive! Down, Watch!' cried Hal, falling down at his feet, with one arm holding down Watch, who tried to lick his face and the King's hand by turns.

'Is it thou, my child, my shepherd?' said Henry, his hands on the lad's head.

'Bless thee! Oh, bless thee, much loved child of my wanderings! I have longed after thee, and prayed for thee, and now God hath given thee to me at this shrine! Kneel and give the Lord thy best thanks, my lad! Ah! how tall thou art! I should not have known thee, Hal, but for Watch.'

'It is well,' muttered Oxford to Musgrave. 'I have not seen him so well nor so cheery all this day. The lad will waken him up and do him good.'

CHAPTER XVII. — A CAPTIVE KING

```
And we see far on holy ground,
  If duly purged our mental view.—KEBLE.
```

The King held Harry Clifford by the hand as he left St. Peter's Church. 'My child, my shepherd boy,' he said, and he called Watch after him, and interested himself in establishing a kind of suspicious peace between the shaggy collie and his own 'Minion,' a small white curly-haired dog, which belonged to a family that had been brought by Queen Margaret from Provence.

His attendant knight, Sir Nicolas Romford, told Sir Giles Musgrave that he had really never seemed so happy since his deliverance, and Sir Nicolas had waited on him ever since his capture, six years previously. He led the youth along to the royal rooms, asking on the way after his sheep and the goodwife who had sent him presents of eggs, then showing him the bullfinch, that greeted his return with loving chirps, and when released from its cage came and sat upon his shoulder and played with his hair, 'A better pet than a fierce hawk, eh, Hal?' he said.

He laughed when he found that Harry thought he had spent all this time in a dark underground dungeon with fetters on his feet.

'Oh no!' he said; 'they were kindly jailors. They dealt better with me than with my Master.'

'Sir, sir, that terrible ride through Cheapside!' said Harry. 'We heard of it at Derwent-side, and we longed to have our pikes at the throats of the villain traitors.'

The King looked as if he hardly remembered that cruel procession, when he was set upon a sorry jade with his feet tied to the stirrups, and shouts of 'Behold the traitor!' around him. Then with a sweet smile of sudden recollection, he said, 'Ah! I recall it, and how I rejoiced to be led in the steps of my Lord, and how the cries sounded, "We will not have this man to reign over us!" Gratias ago, unworthy me, who by my own fault could not reign.'

Harry was silenced, awe-struck, and by-and-by the King took him to see his old chamber in the White Tower, up a winding stone stair. It was not much inferior to the royal lodgings, except in the matter of dais, canopy, and tapestry, and the window looked out into the country, so that the King said he had loved it, and it had many a happy thought connected with it.

Hal followed him in a sort of silent wonder, if not awe, not daring to answer him in monosyllables. This was not quite the hermit of Derwentdale. It was a broader man—not with the breadth of full strength, but of inactivity and advance of years, though the fiftieth year was only lately completed—and the royal robe of crimson, touched with gold, suited him far less than the brown serge of the anchoret. The face was no longer thin, sunburnt, and worn, but pale, and his checks slightly puffed, and the eyes and smile, with more of the strange look of innocent happiness than of old, and of that which seemed to bring back to his young visitor the sense of peace and well-being that the saintly hermit had always given him.

There was consultation that evening between Lord Oxford and Sir Giles Musgrave. It was better, they agreed, to let young Clifford remain with the King as much as possible, but without divulging his name. The King knew it, and indeed had known it, when he received the boy at his hermitage, but he seemed to have forgotten it, as he had much besides. Oxford said that though he could be roused into actual fulfilment of such forms as were required of him, and understood what was set before him, his memory and other powers seemed to have been much impaired, and it was held wiser not to call on him more than could be helped, till the Queen and her son should come to supply the energy that was wanting. They would make the gay and brilliant appearance that the Londoners had admired in Edward of York, and which could not be obtained from poor Henry.

His memory for actual matters was much impaired. Never for two days together could he recollect that his son and Warwick's daughter were married, and it was always by an effort that he remembered that the Prince of Wales was not the eight-years-old child whom he had last seen. As to young Clifford, he sometimes seemed to think the tall nineteen-years-old stripling was just where he had left the child of twelve or thirteen, and if he perceived the age, was so far confused that it was not quite certain that he might not mix him up with his own son, though the knight in constant attendance was sure that he was clear on that point, and only looked on 'Hal' as the child of his teaching and prayers.

But Harry Clifford could not persuade him to enter into that which more and more lay near the youthful heart, the rescuing Anne St. John from the suitor of whom little that was hopeful was heard; and the obtaining her from his father. Of course this could not be unless Harry could win his father's property, and no longer be under the attaint in blood, so as to be able to lay claim to the lands of the De Vescis through his mother; but though the King listened with kindly interest to the story of the children's adventure on the Londesborough moor, and the subsequent meeting in Westmorland, the rescue from the outlaws, and the journey together, it was all like a romance to him—

he would nod his head and promise to do what he could, if he could, but he never remembered it for two days together, and if Hal ventured on anything like pressure, the only answer was, 'Patience, my son, patience must have her work! It is the will of God, it will be right.'

And when Hal began to despair and work himself up and seek to do more with one so impracticable, Lord Oxford and Sir Giles warned him not to force his real name and claims too much, for he did not need too many enemies nor to have Lord St. John and the Nevil who held his lands both anxious to sweep him from their path.

Nor was anything heard from or of the Prioress of Greystone, and whenever the name of George Nevil, the Chancellor and Archbishop of York, was heard, Hal's heart burnt with anxiety, and fear that the lady had forgotten him, though as Dick Nevil, who held the lands of Clifford, was known to be in his suite, it was probable that she was acting out of prudence.

The turmoil of anxious impatience seemed to be quelled when Hal sat on a stool before the King, with Watch leaning against his knee. The instruction or meditation seemed to be taken up much where it had been left six years before, with the same unanswerable questions, only the youth had thought out a great deal more, and the hermit had advanced in a wisdom which was not that of the rough, practical world.

Part of Clifford's day was spent in the tilt-yard, where his two friends, as well as himself, were anxious that he should acquire proficiency and ease such as would become his station, when he recovered it; and a martinet old squire of Oxford proved himself nearly as hard a master as ever Simon Bunce had been.

One very joyous day came to Henry in his regal capacity. Christmas Day had been quietly spent. There was much noisy revelling in the city, and the guards in the castle had their feastings, but Warwick was daily expected to return from France, and neither his brother nor the Archbishop thought that there was much policy in making a public spectacle of a puppet King.

But there was one ceremony from which Henry would not be debarred. He would make the public offering on the Epiphany in Westminster Abbey. He had done so ever since he was old enough to totter up to the altar and hold the offerings; and his heart was set on doing so once more. So a large and quiet cream-coloured Flemish horse was brought for him, he was robed in purple and ermine, with a coronal around the cap that covered his hair, fast becoming white. His train in full array followed him, and the streets were thronged, but there was an ominous lack of applause, and even a few audible jeers at the monk dressed up like the jackdaw in peacock's plumes, and comparisons with

Edward, in sooth a king worth looking at.

Henry seemed not to heed or hear. His blue eyes looked upward, his face was set in peaceful contemplation, his lips were moving, and those who were near enough caught murmurs of 'Vidimus enim stellam Ejus in Oriente et venimus adorare Eum.' Truly the one might be a king to suit the kingdoms of this world, the other had a soul near the Kingdom of Heaven.

The Dean and choir received him at the west door, and with the same rapt countenance he paced up to the sanctuary, and knelt before the chair appropriated to him, while the grand Epiphany Celebration was gone through, in all its glory and beauty of sound and sight, and with the King kneeling with clasped hands, and a radiant look of happiness almost transfiguring that worn face.

When the offertory anthem was sung, he rose up, and advanced to the altar. A salver of gold coins was presented to him, which he took and solemnly laid on the altar, but paused for a moment, and removed his crown with both hands, placing it likewise on the altar, and kneeling for a moment ere he turned to take the vase whence breathed the fragrant odour of frankincense; and presenting this, and afterwards kneeling and bowing low with clasped hands, he again took the salver in which the myrrh was laid. This again he placed on the altar, and remained kneeling in intense devotion through the remainder of the service, only looking up at the 'Sursum Corda,' when those near enough to see his countenance said that they never knew before the full import of those words, nor how the heart could be uplifted.

It was the first time that Hal Clifford had ever joined in the full ceremonial of the Church, or in such splendid accompaniment, for though there had been the rightful ritual at St. Peter's in the Tower, the space had been confined, and the clergy few, and the whole, even on Christmas Day, had been more or less a training to him to enter into what he now saw and heard. He had in these last weeks gathered much of the meaning of all this from the King, who perhaps never fully disentangled the full-grown youth from the boy he had taught at Derwentdale, but who, perhaps for that very cause, really suited better the strange mixture of ignorance, simplicity, observation and aspiration of the shepherd lord.

The King did not help more but less than he had done before in Hal's researches and wonderings about natural objects; he had forgotten the philosophies he had once read, and the supposed circuits of moon, planets and stars only perplexed and worried his brain. It was much more satisfactory to refer all to 'He hath made them fast for ever and ever, He hath given them a law which shall not be broken,' and he could not understand Hal's desire to find out what that law was, and far less his calculations about the tides. He had scarcely ever seen the sea, and as to its motions, 'Hitherto shalt thou come and no farther' was sufficient explanation, and when Hal tried to show him the correspondence between spring tides and full moons he either waved him away or fell asleep.

But on the spiritual side of his mind there was no torpor. He loved to explain the sense of the prayers to his willing pupil, and to tell him the Gospel story, dwelling on whatever could waken or carry on the Christian life; and between the tiltyard and the oratory Hal spent a strange life.

That question which had occurred to him on the journey Hal ventured to lay before his King—'Was it really and truly better and more acceptable worship that came to breathe through him when alone with God under the open vault of Heaven, with endless stars above and beyond, or was the best that which was beautified and guided by priests, with all that man's devices could lavish upon its embellishment?' Such, though in more broken and hesitating words, was the herd boy's difficulty, and Henry put his head back, and after having once said, 'Adam had the one, God directed the other,' he shut his eyes, and Hal feared he would put it aside as he had with the moon and the tides, but after some delay, he leant forward and said, 'My son, if man had always been innocent, that worship as Adam and Eve had it might—nay, would—have sufficed them. The more innocent man is, the better his heart rises. But sin came into the world, and expiation was needed, not only here on earth, but before the just God in Heaven above. Therefore doth He, who hath once offered Himself in sacrifice for us, eternally present His offering in Heaven before the Mercy-Seat, and we endeavour as much as our poor feeble efforts can, to take part in what He does above, and bring it home to our senses by all that can represent to us the glories of Heaven.'

There was much in this that went beyond Hal, who knitted his brow, and would have asked further, but the King fell into a state of contemplation, and noticed nothing, until presently he broke out into a thanksgiving: 'Blessed be my Lord, who hath granted me once more to follow in the steps of the kings of the East, though but as in a dream, and lay my crown and my prayer before Him. Once more I thank Thee, O my true King of kings, and Lord of lords.'

'Oh, do not say once more!' exclaimed Hal. 'Again and again, I trust, sir. It is no dream. It is real.'

The King smiled and shook his head. 'It is all a dream to me,' he said, 'the pageants and the whole. They will not last! Oh, no! It is all but an empty show.'

Hal looked up anxiously, and the King went on: 'Well do I remember the day when, scarce able to walk, and weighed down by my robes, I tottered up to the altar and was well pleased to make my offering, and how my Lord of Warwick, who was then, took me in his arms, and showed me my great father's figure on his grave, and told me I was bound to be such a king as he! Alas! was it mine own error that I so failed?&&

```
Henry born at Monmouth shall short live and gain all,
  Henry born at Windsor shall long live and lose all.'
```

'Oh, sir, sir, do not speak of that old saw!'

Still the King smiled. 'It has come true, my child. All is lost, and it may be well for my soul that thus it should be, and that I should go into the presence of my God freed from the load of what was gained unjustly. I know not whether, if my hand had been stronger, I should have striven to have borne up the burthen of these two realms, but they never ought to have been mine, and if the sins of the forefathers be visited on the children to the third and fourth generation, no marvel that my brain and mine arm could but sink under the weight. Would that I had yielded at once, and spared the bloodshed and sacrilege! Miserere mei! My son was a temptation. Oh, my poor boy! is he to be the heir to all that has come on me? Have pity on him, good Lord!'

'Nay, sir, your brave son will come home to comfort you, and help you and make all well.'

'I know not! I know not! I cannot believe that I shall see him again, or that the visitation of these crimes is not still to come! My son, my sweet son, I can only pray that he might give up his soul sackless and freer of guilt than his father can be, when I remember all that I ought to have hindered when I could think and use my will! Now, now all is but confusion! God has taken away my judgment, even as He did with my French grandsire, and I can only let others act as they will, and pray for them and for myself.'

He had never spoken at such length, nor so clearly, and whenever he was required to come forward, he merely walked, rode, sat or signed rolls as he was told to do, and continually made mistakes as to the persons brought to him, generally calling them by their fathers' names, if he recognised them at all, but still to his nearest attendants, and especially to his beloved herd boy, he was the same gentle, affectionate being, never so happy as at his prayers, and sometimes speaking of holy things as one almost inspired.

CHAPTER XVIII. — AT THE MINORESSES'

The bird that hath been limed in a bush,
  With trembling wings misdoubteth every bush.
  —SHAKESPEARE.

One day, soon after that Twelfth Day, Hal accompanied Sir Giles Musgrave to the shop or stall of Master Lorimer in Cheapside, a wide space, open by day but closed by shutters at night, where all sorts of gilded and emblazoned leather-works for man or horse were displayed, and young 'prentices called, 'What d'ye lack?' 'Saddle of the newest make?' 'Buff coat fit to keep out the spear of Black Douglas himself?'

''Tis Master Lorimer himself I lack,' said Musgrave with a good-humoured smile, and the merchant appeared from a room in the rear, something between a counting-house and a bedroom, where he welcomed his former companions, and insisted on their tasting the good sherris sack that had been sent with his last cargo of Spanish leather.

'I would I could send a flask to our good Prioress,' he said, 'to cheer her heart. I went to the Minoresses' as she bade me, to settle some matters of account with her, and after some ado, Sister Mabel came down to the parlour and told me the Prioress is very sick with a tertian fever, and they misdoubt her recovering.'

'And the young Lady of St. John.'

'She is well enough, but sadly woeful as to the Mother Prioress, and likewise as to what they hear of the Lord Redgrave. It is the old man, not his son, a hard and stark old man, as I remember. He would have bargained with me for the coats of the poor rogues slain at St. Albans, and right evil was his face as he spoke thereof, he being then for Queen Margaret; but then he went over to King Edward, and glutted himself with slaughter at Towton, and here he calls himself Red Rose again. Ill-luck to the poor young maid if she falls to him!'

It was terrible news for Hal, and Musgrave could not but gratify him by riding by the Minories to endeavour to hear further tidings of the Prioress.

It was a grand building in fine pointed architecture, for the Clares, though once poor, in imitation of St. Clara and St. Francis, had been dispensed collectively from their vow of poverty, and though singly incapable of holding property, had a considerable accumulation en masse. They were themselves a strict Order, but they often gave lodgings to ladies either in retreat or for any cause detained near London.

Sir Giles and Harry were only admitted to the outer court, whence the portress went with their message of inquiry. They waited a long time, and then the Greystone lay Sister who had been the companion of their journey came back in company with the portress.

'Benedicite, dear gentles,' she said; 'oh, you are a sight for sair een.'

'And how fares the good Mother Prioress?' asked the Lord of Peelholm.

'Alack! she is woefully ill when the fever takes her, and she is wasted away so that you would scarce know her; but this is one of the better days, and if you, sir, will come into the parlour, she will see you. She was arraying herself as I came down. She was neither to have nor to hold when she heard you were there, and said a north country face would be better to her than all the Sisters' potions!'

They were accordingly conducted through a graceful cloister, overgrown with trailing ivy, to a bare room, with mullioned windows, and frescoes on the Walls with the history of St. Francis relieving beggars, preaching to the birds, &c., and with a stout open work barrier cutting off half the room.

Presently the Prioress tottered in, leaning heavily on the arms of Sister Mabel and of Anne St. John, while her own lay Sister and another placed a seat for her; but before she would sit down, she would go up to the opening, and turning back her veil, put out a hand to be grasped. 'Right glad am I to see you, good Sir Giles and young Harry. Are you going back to the wholesome winds of our moors?'

'Not yet, holy Mother. It grieves me to see you faring so ill.'

'Ah! a breeze from the north would bring life back to my old bones. Aye, Giles, this place has made an old woman of me.' And truly her bright ruddy face was faded to a purple hue, and her cheeks hung haggard and almost withered, but as her visitors expressed their grief and sympathy, she went on in her own tone. 'And tell me somewhat of how things are going. How doth Richard of Warwick comport himself to the King? Hath your King zest enough to reign? Is my White Rose King still abroad in Burgundy?' And as Sir Giles replied to each inquiry in turn, and told all he could of political matters, she exclaimed: 'Ah! that is better than the hearing whether the black hen hath laid an egg, or the skein of yellow silk matches. I am weary, O! I am weary. Moreover, young Hal, I know as matters are that could I see George Nevil face to face I could do somewhat with him, and I laid my plans to obtain a meeting, but therewith, what with vexation and weariness and lack of air, comes this sickness, and I am laid aside and can do nought but pray, and lay my plans to meet him some day in the fields, and show him what a hawk can do, then shame him into listening to my tale. But I must be a sound woman first! And maybe his brother Warwick, being a sturdy gentleman who loves a brave man, will be better to deal with. I am a sinful woman, and maybe my devotions here will help me to be more worthy to be heard. Moreover, I hoped you had done somewhat in thine own cause with thy King and Earl Oxford,' she proceeded. 'Thou hast an esquire's coat; hast thou any hope of thy lands?'

'I must strive to earn them by deeds,' said Hal. 'And—'

'Well spoken, lad! 'Tis the manly way; but methought you hadst interest with this King of thine, or hath he only a royal memory for services?'

'He is good to me. Yea, most good,' began Harry.

'Ay, he loves the boy,' said Sir Giles, 'no question about that; but his memory for all that is about him hath failed, and there is nothing for it save to wait for the Queen and the Prince, who will bear the boy's father's services in mind.'

'And wherefore tarries the French woman? This maid's father is to come over with her. He is forming her English court, I trow; she can have few beside from England.'

'When he comes,' said Harry, with a look into Anne's eyes that made them droop and her cheeks burn, 'then shall we put it to the touch. Then shall I know whether I have mine own, and what is more than mine own.'

'Thine own,' whispered Anne. 'Oh, better live in the sheepfolds with thee than with this Baron! I shudder at the thought.'

This, and a few more such words were an aside, while the Prioress continued her conversation with Sir Giles, and went on to say that she was sure she should never recover till she was out of these walls, and away from London smoke and London smells, and she naughtily added in a whisper the weary talk of these good nuns, who had never flown a hawk or chased a deer in their lives, and thought Florimond a mere wolf, if not the evil one himself, and kept the poor hound chained up like a malefactor in gyves, till she was fain to send him away with Master Lorimer to keep for her.

She would not go back to her Priory till Anne's fate was settled, being in hopes of doing something yet for the poor wench; but meantime she should die if she stayed there much longer, and she meant to set forth on pilgrimage in good time, before she had scandalised the good ladies enough to make them gossip to the dames of St. Helen's, who would be only too glad to have a story against the Benedictines. A ride over the Kentish downs was the only cure for her or for Anne, who had been pining ever since they had been mewed up here, though, looking across at the girl, whose head was leaning against the bars, Sir Giles seemed to have brought a remedy to judge by those cheeks.

'Would that we could hope it would be an effectual and lasting remedy,' sighed Sir Giles; 'but unless this poor King could be roused to insist, or the Earl of Warwick fell out with his cousin, I do not see much chance for the lad.'

'Is it Warwick who is his chief foe or King Edward?' asked the Prioress.

'King Edward, doubtless, for his father's slaughter of young Rutland at Wakefield.'

'That bodes ill,' said the lady. 'By all I gather, King Edward is a tiger when once roused, but at other times is like that same tiger, purring and slow to move. But there's a bell that warns us to vespers. They are mightily more strict here than ever we are at Greystone. Ah! you won't tell tales, Sir Giles! You'll soon hear of me at St. Thomas's shrine at Canterbury.'

The knight took his leave. It was impossible not to like and pity the Prioress, though the life among devout nuns was clearly beyond her powers.

The dreamy peaceful days of the Tower of London were stirred by the arrival of the great Earl of Warwick, the Kingmaker, as people already called him. He took up his residence in his own mighty establishment at Warwick House near St. Paul's; and the day after his arrival, he came clanking over London Bridge with a great following of knights and squires to pay his respects to King Henry.

Henry Clifford was not disposed to meet him, and only watched from a window when the drawbridge was lowered, and the sturdy man, with grizzled hair and marked, determined features, rode into the gateway, where he was received by the Earl of Oxford.

The interview was long, and when it was finished, the two Earls made the round of the defences, and Oxford drew up his garrison on the Tower Green to be inspected.

When Warwick had taken his leave, Hal was summoned to the Constable's hall. 'We must be jogging, my young master,' he said. 'There are rumours of King Edward making another attempt for his crown, and my Lord of Warwick would have me go and watch the eastern seaboard. And you had best go with me.'

'The King—' began Hal.

'You will come back to the King by-and-by if so be he misses you, but he was more dazed than ever to-day, and perhaps it was well, for Warwick brought with him Dick Nevil, who has got your lands of Clifford, and might be tempted to put you out of the way in one of the dungeons that lie so handy.'

'No one save the King knows who I am,' said Hal, 'and he forgets from day to day all save that I am the herd boy, and I think it cheers him to have me with him. I will stay beside him even as a varlet.'

'Nay, my lord, that may not be. 'Tis true he loves thee, but he will forget anon, and I may not suffer the risk. Too many know or guess.'

Harry Clifford repeated that he recked not of the risk when he could serve and comfort his beloved King, and, indeed, his mind was made up on the subject. He had taken measures for remaining as one of the men-at-arms of the garrison; but King Henry himself surprised him by saying, 'My young Lord of Clifford, fare thee well. Thou goest forth to-morrow with the Constable of Oxford. Take my blessing with thee, my child. Thou hast been granted to me to make life very sweet to me of late, and I thank God for it, but the time is come that thou must part from me.'

'Oh, sir, never! None was ever so dear to me! For weal or woe I will be with you! Suffer me to be your meanest varlet, and serve you as none other can do.'

Henry shook his head. 'It may not be, my child, let not thy blood also be on my head! Go with Oxford and his men. Thou hast learnt to draw sword and use lance. Thou wilt be serving me still if again there be, which Heaven forefend, stricken fields in my cause or my son's.'

'Sir, if I must fight, let no less holy hand than thine lay knighthood on my shoulder,' sobbed Hal, kneeling.

Henry smiled. 'I have well-nigh forgotten the fashion. But if it will please thee, my son, give me thy sword, Oxford. In the name of God and St. George of England I dub thee knight. For the Church, for the honour of God, for a good cause, fight. Arise, Sir Henry Clifford!'

CHAPTER XIX. — A STRANGE EASTER EVE

```
And spare, O spare
   The meek usurper's holy head.
   —GRAY.
```

Once more, at the close of morning service, while it was still dark, did Harry Clifford, the new-made knight, kneel before King Henry and feel his hand in blessing on his head. Then he went forth to join Musgrave and the troop that the Earl of Oxford was leading from the Tower to raise the counties of East Anglia and watch the coast against a descent of King Edward from the Low Countries.

As they passed the walls enclosing the Minories Convent, and Hal gazed at it wistfully, the wide gateway was opened and out came a party of black-hooded nuns, mounted on ponies and mules, evidently waiting till Oxford's band had gone by. Harry drew Sir Giles's attention, and they lingered, as they became certain that they beheld the Prioress Selby of Greystone, hawk, hound and all, riding forth, nearly smothered in her hood, and not so upright as of old.

'Ay, here I am!' she said, as he reined up and bowed his greeting. 'Here I am on my pilgrimage! I got Father Ridley, the Benedictine head, to order me forth. Methinks he was glad, being a north countryman, to send me out before I either died on the Poor Clares' hands, or gave them a fuller store of tales against us of St. Bennet's! Not but that they are good women, too godly and devout for a poor wild north country Selby like me, who cannot live without air.

```
O the oak and the ash and the bonny ivy tree,
   They flourish best at home in the north countree.
```

Flori, Flori, whither away? Ah! thou hast found thine old friend. Birds of a feather. Eh? the young folk have foregathered likewise. Watch! And thou, sir knight, whither are you away?'

'On our way to Norfolk in case the Duke of York should show himself on the coast. And yours, reverend Mother?'

'To Canterbury first by easy journeys. We sleep to-night at the Tabard, where we shall meet other pilgrims.'

'Here, alack! our way severs from yours. Farewell, holy Mother, may you find health on your pilgrimage.'

'Every breath I take in is health,' said the Mother, who had already manoeuvred an opening in her veil, and gasped to throw it back as soon as she should attain an unfrequented place. 'There are so many coming and going here that all the air is used up by their greasy nostrils! Well! good luck, and God's blessing go with you, and you, young Hal, I may say so far, whichever side ye be, but still I hold that York has the right, and yours may be a saint, but not a king.'

Hal had meantime 'forgathered' as the Prioress said with Anne, marching, in spite of his new honours, close to her stirrup, and venturing to whisper to her that he was now her knight, and 'her colours,' which he was to wear for her, were only a tiny scrap of ribbon from her glove, which he cut off with his dagger, and kissed, saying he should wear it next his heart, though he might not do so openly.

Their love was more implied than ever it had been before, and she repeated her confidence that the kind Prioress would never leave her till she had done her utmost for them both.

'But you, my good stripling, I am ashamed to see you. I have done nothing for you. I sent a humble message to ask to see the Archbishop, but had no answer, and by-and-by, when I stirred again, who should come to see me but young Bertram Selby, and "Kinswoman," said he, "you had best keep quiet. The Archbishop hath asked me whether rumours were sooth that yours was scarce a regular Priory." The squire stood up for me and said, as became one of the family, that an outlying cell, where there were ill neighbours of Scots, thieves, borderers, and the like, could scarce look to be as trim as a city nunnery, and that none had ever heard harm of Mother Agnes. But then one of his priests took on him to whisper in his ear, and he demanded whether we had not gone so far as to hide traitors from justice, to which Bertram returned a stout denial as well he might, though he thought it well to give me warning, but for the present there was no use in attempting anything more. The Archbishop was exceedingly busy with the work of his office and the defence of London in case of Edward's threatened return; but he had not yet come, and no one thought there was a reasonable doubt that Warwick, the Kingmaker, would not be victorious, and he had carried his son-in-law, the Duke of Clarence, with him.' After the cause of the Red Rose was won, there was no fear but that the services of Clifford would be remembered. So Harry Clifford parted with Anne, promising himself and her that there should be fresh Clifford services, winning a recognition of the De Vesci inheritance if of no more.

The ladies went on their way in the track which Chaucer has made memorable, laying their count to meet Queen Margaret and her son, and win their ears beforehand, and wondering that they came not. Kentish breezes soon revived the Prioress, and she went through many strange devotions at the shrine of Becket, which, it might be feared, did not improve her spiritual, so much as her bodily, health, while Anne's chiefly resolved themselves into prayers that Harry Clifford might be guarded and restored, and that she herself might be saved from the dreaded Lord Redgrave.

They did not set out on the return to London till they had inhaled plenty of sea breezes by visiting the shrine of St. Mildred in the isle of Thanet, and St. Eanswith at Folkestone, till Lent had begun, and the first fresh tidings that they met were that Edward had landed in Yorkshire, but his fleet had been dispersed by storms, and the people did not rise to join him, so that he was fain to proclaim that he only came to assert his right to his father's inheritance of the Dukedom of York.

At the Minoresses' Convent they found that a messenger had arrived, bidding Anne go to meet her father at his castle in Bedfordshire. He was coming over with the Queen whenever she could obtain a convoy from King Louis of France. Lord Redgrave was with him, and the marriage should take place as soon as they arrived.

'Never fear, child,' said the Prioress; 'many is the slip between the cup and the lip.'

Further tidings came that Edward had thrown off his first plea, that he had passed Warwick's brother Montagu at Pontefract, and that men from his own hereditary estates were flocking to his royal banner. Warwick was calling up his men in all directions, and both armies were advancing on London. Then it was known that 'false, fleeting, perjured Clarence' had deserted his father-in-law, and returned to his brother; and worthless as he individually was, it boded ill for Lancaster, though still hope continued in the uniform success of the Kingmaker. Warwick was about twenty miles in advance of Edward, till that King actually passed him and reached the town of Warwick itself. Still the Earl wrote to his brother that if he could only hold out London for forty- eight hours all would be well.

Once more poor King Henry was set on horseback and paraded through the streets. Brother Martin went out with the chaplain of the Poor Clares to gaze upon him, and they came back declaring that he was more than ever like the image carried in a procession, seeming quite as helpless and indifferent, except, said Brother Martin, when he passed a church, and then a heavenly look came over his still features as he bowed his head; but none of the crowd who came out to gaze cried 'Save King Harry!' or 'God bless him!'

There were two or three thousand Yorkists in the various sanctuaries of London, and they were preparing to rise in favour of their King Edward, and only a few hundred were mustering in St. Paul's Churchyard for the Red

Rose.

The Poor Clares were in much terror, though nunneries and religious houses, and indeed non-combatants in general, were usually respected by each side in these wars; but the Prioress of Greystone was not sorry that the summons to her protegee called her party off on the way to Bedfordshire, and they all set forward together, intending to make Master Lorimer's household at Chipping Barnet their first stage, as they had engaged to do.

Their intention had been notified to Lorimer's people in his London shop, who had sent on word to their master, and the good man came out to meet them, full of surprise at the valour of the ladies in attempting the journey. But they could not possibly go further. King Edward was at St. Albans, and was on his way to London, and the Earl of Warwick was coming up from Dunstable with the Earls of Somerset and Oxford. For ladies, even of religious orders, to ride on between the two hosts was manifestly impossible, and he and his wife were delighted to entertain the Lady Prioress till the roads should be safe.

The Prioress was nothing loth. She always enjoyed the freedom of a secular household, and she was glad to remain within hearing of the last news in this great crisis of York and Lancaster.

'I marvel if there will be a battle,' she said. 'Never have I had the good luck to see or hear one.'

'Oh! Mother, are you not afraid?' cried Sister Mabel.

'Afraid! What should I be afraid of, silly maid? Do you think the men-at-arms are wolves to snap you up?'

'And,' murmured Anne, 'we shall know how it goes with my Lord of Oxford's people.'

These were the last days of Lent, and were carefully kept in the matter of food by the household, but the religious observances were much disturbed by the tidings that poured in. King Henry and Archbishop Nevil had taken refuge in the house of Bishop Kemp of London, Urswick the Recorder, with the consent of the Aldermen, had opened the gates to Edward, and the Good Friday Services at Barnet, the Psalms and prayers in the church, were disturbed by men-at-arms galloping to and fro, and reports coming in continually.

There could be no going out to gather flowers to deck the Church the next day, for King Edward was on the London side, and Warwick with his army had reached the low hills of Hadley, and their tents, their banners, and the glint of their armour might be seen over the heathy slope between them and the lanes and fields, surrounded by hedges, that fenced in the valley of Barnet. The little town itself, though lying between the two armies, remained unoccupied by either party, and only men-at-arms came down into it, not as plunderers, but to buy food.

Warwick's cannon, however, thundered all night, a very awful sound to such unaccustomed ears, but they were so directed that the charges flew far away from Barnet, under a false impression as to the situation of the Yorkist forces.

Mistress Lorimer had heard them before, but accompanied every report with a pious prayer; Sister Mabel screamed at each, then joined in; the Prioress was greatly excited, and walked about with Master Lorimer, now on the roof, trying to see, now at the gate, trying to hear. Anne fancied it meant victory to Hal's party, but knelt, tried to pray while she listened, and the dogs barked incessantly. And that Hal must be in the army above the little town they guessed, for in the evening Watch came floundering into the courtyard, hungry and muddy, but full of affectionate recognition of his old friends and the quarters he had learnt to know. Florimond, who happened to be loose, had a romp with him in their old fashion, and to the vexation and alarm of his mistress, they both ran off together, and must have gone hunting on the heath, for there was no response to her silver whistle.

CHAPTER XX. — BARNET

A dead hush fell; but when the dolorous day
  Grew drearier toward twilight falling, came
A bitter wind, clear from the North, and blew
The mist aside.
—TENNYSON.

And Sir Henry Clifford? Still he was Hal of Derwentdale, for the perilous usurper, Sir Richard Nevil, was known to be continually with Warwick, and Musgrave was convinced that the concealment was safest.

The youth then remained with the Peelholm men, and became a good deal more practised in warlike affairs, and accustomed to campaigning, during the three months when Oxford was watching the eastern coast. On this Easter night he lay down on the hill-side with Watch beside him, his shepherd's plaid round him, his heart rising as he thought himself near upon gaining fame and honour wherewith to win his early love, and winning victory and safety for his beloved King, or rather his hermit. For as his hermit did that mild unearthly face always come before him. He could not think of it wearing that golden crown, which seemed alien to it, but rather, as he lay on his back, after his old habit looking up at the stars, either he saw and recognised the Northern Crown, or his dazed and sleepy fancy wove a radiant coronet of stars above that meek countenance that he knew and loved so well; and as at intervals the cannon boomed and wakened him, he looked on at the bright Northern Cross and dreamily linked together the cross and crown.

Easter Sunday morning came dawning, but no one looked to see the sun dance, even if the morning had not been dull and grey, a thick fog covering everything; but through it came a dull and heavy sound, and the clang of armour. Even by their own force the radiant star of the De Veres could hardly be seen on the banner, as the Earl of Oxford rode up and down, putting his men in battle array. Hal was on foot as an archer, meaning to deserve the spurs that he had not yet worn. The hosts were close to one another, and at first only the continual rain of arrows darkened the air; but as the sun rose and the two armies saw one another, Oxford's star was to be seen carried into the very midst of the opposing force under Lord Hastings. On, on, with cries of victory, the knights rode, the archers ran across the heath carrying all before them, never doubting that the day was theirs, but not knowing where they were till trumpets sounded, halt was called, and they were drawn up together, as best they might, round their leading star. But as they advanced, behold there was an unexpected shout of treason. Arrows came thickly on them, men-at-arms bearing Warwick's ragged staff came thundering headlong upon them. 'Treason, treason,' echoed on all sides, and with that sound in his ears

Harry Clifford was cut down, and fell under a huge horse and man, and lay senseless under a gorse-bush.

He knew no more but that horses and men seemed for ever trampling over him and treading him down, and then all was lost to him—for how long he knew not, but for one second he was roused so far as to hear a furious growling and barking of Watch, but with dazed senses he thought it was over the sheep, tried to raise himself, could not, thought himself dying, and sank back again.

The next thing he knew was 'Here, Master Lorimer, you know this gear better than I; unfasten this buff coat. There, he can breathe. Drink this, my lad.'

It was the Prioress's voice! He felt a jolt as of a waggon, and opened his eyes. It was dark, but he knew he was under the tilt of Lorimer's waggon, which was moving on. The Prioress was kneeling over him on one side, Lorimer on the other, and his head was on a soft lap—nay, a warm tear dropped on his face, a sweet though stifled voice said, 'Is he truly better?'

Then came sounds of 'hushing,' yet of reassurance; and when there was a halt, and clearer consciousness began to revive, while kind hands were busy about him, and a cordial was poured down his throat, by the light of a lantern cautiously shown, Hal found speech to say, as he felt a long soft tongue on his face, 'Watch, Watch, is it thou, man?'

'Ay, Watch it is,' said the Prioress. 'Well may you thank him! It is to him you owe all, and to my good Florimond.'

'But what—how—where am I?' asked Hal, trying to look round, but feeling sharp thrills and shoots of pain at every motion.

'Lie still till they bring their bandages, and I will tell you. Gently, Nan, gently—thy sobs shake him!' But, as he managed to hold and press Anne's hand, the Prioress went on, 'You are in good Lorimer's warehouse. Safer thus, though it is too odorous, for the men of York do not respect sanctuary in the hour of victory.'

The word roused Hal further. 'The victory was ours!' he said. 'We had driven Hastings' banner off the field! Say, was there a cry of treason?'

'Even so, my son. So far as Master Lorimer understands, Lord Oxford's banner of the beaming star was mistaken for the sun of York, and the men of Warwick turned on you as you came back from the chase, but all was utter confusion. No one knows who was staunch and who not, and the fields and lanes are full of blood and slaughtered men; and Edward's royal banner is set up on the market cross, and trumpets were sounding round it. And here come

Master Lorimer and the goodwife to bind these wounds.'

'But Sir Giles Musgrave?' still asked Hal.

'Belike fled with Lord Oxford and his men, who all made off at the cry of treason,' was the answer.

Lorimer returned with his wife and various appliances, and likewise with fresh tidings. There was no doubt that the brothers Warwick and Montagu had been slain. They had been found—Warwick under a hedge impeded by his heavy armour, and Montagu on the field itself. Each body had been thrown over a horse, and shown at the market cross; and they would be carried to London on the morrow. 'And so end,' said Lorimer, 'two brave and open-handed gentlemen as ever lived, with whom I have had many friendly dealings.'

One thing more Hal longed to hear—namely, how he had been saved. He remembered that Watch had come back to him with Florimond the evening before. They had probably been hunting together, and the hound, who had always been very fond of him on the journey, had accompanied Watch to his side before going back to his chain in Barnet; but he had lost sight of them in the morning, and regretted that he could not find Watch to provide for his safety. He knew, he said, by the presence of Florimond, who must be in Barnet. And he also had a dim recollection of being licked by Watch's tongue as he lay, and likewise of hearing a furious barking, yelling and growling, whether of one or both dogs he was not sure.

It seemed that towards the evening, when the battle-cries had grown fainter, and the sun was going down, Florimond had burst in on his mistress, panting and blood-stained—but not with his own blood, as was soon ascertained—and made vehement demonstrations by which, as a true dog-lover, the Prioress perceived that he wanted her to follow him. And Anne, who thought she saw a piece of Hal's plaid caught in his collar, was 'neither to have nor to hold,' as the Mother said, till Master Lorimer was found, and entreated to follow the hound, ay, and to take them with him. He demurred much as to their safety, but the Prioress declared that it was the part of the religious to take care of the wounded, and not inconsistent with her vow. See the Sisters of St. Katharine's of the Tower! And though her interpretation was a broad one, and would have shocked alike her own Abbess and her of the Minoresses, he was fain to accept it in such a cause; but he commanded his waggoners to bring the wain in the rear, both as an excuse, and a possible protection for the ladies, and, it might be, a conveyance for the wounded.

Florimond, who had sprung about, barked, fawned and made entreating sounds all this time (longer in narrative than in reality) led them, not through the central field of slaughter, but somewhat to the left, among the heath—where, in fact, Oxford had lost his way in the fog, and his own allies had charged him, but had not followed far beyond the place of Hal's fall, discovering the fatal error that spread confusion through their ranks, where everyone distrusted his fellow leader.

There, after a weary and perilous way, diversified by the horrid shouts of plunderers of the slain, happily not near at hand, and when Lorimer, but for the ladies, would have given up the quest as useless, they were greeted by Watch's bark, and found him lying with his fine head alert and ready over his senseless master.

There was no doubt but that the two good creatures, both powerful and formidable animals, must have saved him from the spoilers, and then been sagacious enough to let the hound go down to fetch assistance while the sheep-dog remained as his master's faithful guardian. How honoured and caressed they were can hardly be described, but all will know.

The joy and gratitude of knowing of Anne's devotion, and the pleasure of his good dog's faithfulness, helped Hal through the painful process of having his hurts dealt with. Surgeons, even barbers, were fully occupied, and Lorimer did not wish to have it known that a Lancastrian was in his house. His wife and her old nurse, as well as the Prioress, had some knowledge of simple practical surgery; and Hal's disasters proved to be a severe cut on the head, a slash on the shoulder, various bruises, and a broken rib and thigh-bone, all which were within their capabilities, with assistance from the master's stronger hand. No one could tell whether the savage nature of the York brothers might not slake their revenge in a general massacre of their antagonists; so Lorimer caused Hal's bed to be made in the waggon in the warehouse, where he was safe from detection until the victorious army should have quitted Barnet.

CHAPTER XXI. — TEWKESBURY

The last shoot of that ancient tree
    Was budding fair as fair might be;
        Its buds they crop
        Its branches lop
    Then leave the sapless stem to die.
—SOPHOCLES (Anstice).

Harry Clifford lay fevered, and knowing little of what passed, for several days, only murmuring sometimes of his flock at home, sometimes of the royal hermit, and sometimes in distress of the men-at-arms with whom he had been thrown, and whose habits and language had plainly been a great shock to his innocent mind, trained by the company of the sheep, and the hermit. He took the Prioress's hand for Good-wife Dolly's, but he generally knew Anne, who could soothe him better than any other.

Master Lorimer was fully occupied by combatants who came to have their equipments renewed or repaired, and he spent the days in his shop in London, but rode home in the long evenings with his budget of news. King Henry was in the Tower again, as passive as ever, but on the very day of the battle of Barnet Queen Margaret had landed at Weymouth with her son, and the war would be renewed in Somersetshire.

Search for prisoners being over at Barnet, Hal was removed to the guest chamber of his hosts, where he lay in a huge square bed, and in the better air began to recover, understand what was going on round him, and be anxious for his friends, especially Sir Giles Musgrave and Simon Bunce. The ladies still attended to him, as Lorimer pronounced the journey to be absolutely unsafe, while so many soldiers disbanded, or on their way to the Queen's army, were roaming about, and the Burgundians brought by Edward might not be respectful to an English Prioress. It was safer to wait for tidings from Lord St. John, which were certain to come either from Bletso or the Minoresses'.

So May had begun when Lorimer hurried home with the tidings that a messenger had come in haste from King Edward from the battlefield of Tewkesbury, with the tidings of a complete victory. Prince Edward, the fair and spirited hope of Lancaster, was slain, Somerset and his friends had taken sanctuary in the Abbey Church, Queen Margaret and the young wife of the prince in a small convent, and beyond all had been flight and slaughter.

For a few days no more was known, but then came fuller and sadder tidings. The young prince had been brutally slain by his cousins, Edward, George, and Richard, excited as they were to tiger-like ferocity by the late revolt. The nobles in the sanctuary, who had for one night been protected by a cord drawn in front of them by a priest, had in the morning been dragged out and beheaded. Among them was Anne's father, Lord St. John of Bletso, and on the field the heralds had recognised the corpse of her suitor, Lord Redgrave. To expect that Anne felt any acute sorrow for a father whom she had never seen since she was six years old, and who then had never seemed to care for her, was not possible.

And what was to be her fate? Her young brother, the heir of Bletso, was in Flanders with his foreign mother, and she knew not what might be her own claims through her own mother, though the Prioress and Master Lorimer knew that it could be ascertained through the seneschal at Bletso, if he had not perished with his lord, or the agents at York through whom Anne's pension had been paid. If she were an heiress, she would become a ward of the Crown, a dreary prospect, for it meant to be disposed of to some unknown minion of the Court.

CHAPTER XXII. — THE NUT-BROWN MAID

```
All my wellfare to trouble and care
    Should change if you were gone,
For in my mynde, of all mankind
    I love but you alone.
-NUT-BROWN MAID.
```

Anne St. John, in her 'doul' or deep mourning, sat by Hal's couch or daybed in tears, as he lay in the deep bay of the mullioned window, and told him of the consultation that had been held.

'Ah, dear lady!' he said, 'now am I grieved that I have not mine own to endow you with! Well would I remain the landless shepherd were it not for you.'

'Nay,' she said, looking up through her tears, 'and wherefore should I not share your shepherd's lot?'

'You! Nan, sweet Nan, tenderly nurtured in the convent while I have ever lived as a rough hardy shepherd!'

'And I have ever been a moorland maid,' she answered, 'bred to no soft ways. I know not how to be the lady of a castle—I shall be a much better herdsman's wife, like your good old Dolly, whom I have always loved and envied.'

'You never saw us snowed up in winter with all things scarce, and hardly able to milk a goat.'

'Have not we been snowed up at Greystone for five weeks at a time?'

'Ay, but with thick walls round and a stack of peat at hand,' said Hal, his heart beating violently as more and more he felt that the maiden did not speak in jest, but in full earnestness of love.

'Verily one would deem you took me for a fine dainty dame, such as I saw at the Minoresses', shivering at the least gust of fresh wind, and not daring to wet their satin shoes if there had been a shower of rain in the cloisters. Were we not all stifled within the walls, and never breathed till we were out of them? Nay, Hal, there is none to come between us now. Take me to your moors and hills! I will be your good housewife and shepherdess, and make you such a home! And you will teach me of the stars and of the flowers and all the holy lore of your good royal hermit.'

'Ah! my hermit, my master, how fares it with him? Would that I could go and see!'

'Which do you love best—me or the hermit?' asked Anne archly, lifting up her head, which was lying on his shoulder.

'I love you, mine own love and sweetheart, with all my heart,' he said, regaining her hand, 'but my King and master with my soul; and oh! that I had any strength to give him! I love him as my master in holy things, and as my true prince, and what would I not give to know how it is with him and how he bears these dreadful tidings!'

He bent his head, choking with sobs as he spoke, and Anne wept with him, her momentary jealousy subdued by the picture of the lonely prisoner, his friends slain in his cause, and his only child cut off in early prime; but she tried the comfort of hoping that his Queen would be with him. Thus talking now of love, now of grief, now of the future, now of the past, the Prioress found them, and as she was inclined to blame Anne for letting her patient weep, the maiden looked up to her and said, 'Dear Mother, we are disputing
—I want this same Hal to wed me so soon as he can stand and walk. Then I would go home with him to Derwentside, and take care of him.'

The Prioress burst out laughing. 'Make porridge, milk the ewes and spin their wool? Eh? Meet work for a baron's daughter!'

'So I tell her,' said Harry. 'She knows not how hard the life is.'

'Do I not?' said Anne. 'Have I not spent a night and day, the happiest my childhood knew, in your hut? Has it not been a dream of joy ever since?'

'Ay, a summer's dream!' said Hal. 'Tell her the folly of it.'

'I verily believe he does not want me. If he had not a lame leg, I trow he would be trying to be mewed up with his King!'

'It would be my duty,' murmured Hal, 'nor should I love thee the less.'

''Tis a duty beyond your reach,' said the Prioress. 'Master Lorimer hears that none have access to King Henry, God help him! and he sits as in a trance, as though he understood and took heed of nothing—not even of this last sore battle.'

'God aid him! Aye, and his converse is with Him,' said Hal, with a gush of tears. 'He minds nought of earth, not even earthly griefs.'

'But we, we are of earth still, and have our years before us,' said Anne, 'and I will not spend mine the dreary lady of a dull castle. Either I will back and take my vows in your Priory, reverend Mother, if Hal there disdains to have me.'

'Nan, Nan! when you know that all I dread is to have you mewed behind a wall of snow as thick as the walls of the Tower and freezing to the bone!'

'With you behind it telling all the tales. Mother, prithee prove to him that I am not made of sugar like the Clares, but that I love a fresh wind and the open moorlands.'

The Prioress laughed and took her away, but in private the maiden convinced her that the proposal, however wild, was in full earnest, and not in utter ignorance of the way of life that was preferred.

Afterwards the good lady discussed it with the Lorimers. 'For my part,' she said, 'I see nought to gainsay the children having their way. They are equal in birth and breeding, and love one another heartily, and the times may turn about to bring them to their own proper station.'

'But the hardness and the roughness of the life,' objected Mistress Lorimer, 'for a dainty, convent-bred lady.'

'My convent—God, forgive me!—is not like the Poor Clares. We knew there what cold and hunger mean, as well as what free air and mountains are. Moreover, though the maid thinks not of it, I do not believe the life will be so bare and comfortless. The lad's mother hath not let him want, and there is a heritage through the Vescis that must come to him, even if he never can claim the lands of Clifford.'

'And now that all Lancaster is gone, King Edward may be less vindictive against the Red Rose,' said Lorimer.

'There must be a dowry secured to the maid,' said the Prioress. 'Let them only lie quiet for a time till the remains of the late tempest have blown over, and all will be well with them. Ay, and Master Lorimer, the Lady Threlkeld, as well as myself, will fully acquit ourselves of the heavy charges you have been put to for your hospitality to us.'

Master Lorimer disclaimed all save his delight in the honour paid to his poor house, and appealed to his wife, who seconded him courteously, though perhaps the expenses of a wounded knight, three nuns, a noble damsel and their horses, were felt by her enough to make the promise gratifying.

While the elders talked, a horseman was heard in the court, asking whether the young demoiselle of Bletso were lodged there. It was the seneschal Wenlock, who had come with what might be called the official report of his lord's death, and to consider of the disposal of the young lady, being glad to find the Prioress of Greystone, to whom she had originally been committed by her father.

Before summoning her, he explained to the Prioress that a small estate which had belonged to her mother devolved upon her. The proceeds of the property were not large, but they had been sufficient to keep her at the convent, on the moderate charges of the time. Anne was only eighteen, and at no time of their lives were women, even widows, reckoned able to dispose of themselves. She would naturally become a ward of the Crown, and Lord Redgrave having been killed, the seneschal was about to go and inform King Edward of the situation.

'But,' said the Prioress, 'suppose you found her already betrothed to a gentleman of equal birth, and with claims to an even greater inheritance? Would you not be silent till the match was concluded, and the King had no chance of breaking it?'

'If it were well for the maid's honour and fortune,' said the seneschal. 'If you, reverend Mother, have found a fair marriage for her, it might be better to let well alone.'

Then the Prioress set forth the situation and claims of young Clifford, and the certainty, that even if it were more prudent not to advance them at present, yet the ruin of the house of Nevil removed one great barrier, and at least the Vesci inheritance held by his mother must come to him, and she was the more likely to make a portion over to him when she found that he had married nobly.

The seneschal acquiesced, even though the Prioress confessed that the betrothal had not actually taken place. In fact he was relieved that the maiden, whom he had known as a fair child, should be off his hands, and secured from the greed of some Yorkist partisan needing a reward.

When Anne, her dark eyes and hair shaded by her mourning veil, came down, and had heard his greeting, with such details of her father's death and the state of the family as he could give her, she rose and said: 'Sir, there have been passages between Sir Harry Clifford and myself, and I would wed none other than him.'

Nor did the seneschal gainsay her.

All that he desired was that what was decided upon should be done quickly, before heralds or lawyers brought to the knowledge of the Woodvilles that there was any sort of prize to be had in the damsel of St. John, and he went off, early the next morning, back to Bletso, that he might seem to know nothing of the matter.

The Prioress laughed at men being so much more afraid than women. She was willing to bear all the consequences, but then the Plantagenets were not in the habit of treating ladies as traitors. However, all agreed that it would be wiser to be out of reach of London as soon as possible, and Master Lorimer, who had become deeply interested in this romance of true love, arranged to send one of his wains to York, in which the bride and bridegroom might travel unsuspected, until the latter should be able to ride and all were out of reach of pursuit. The Prioress would go thus far with them, 'And then! And then,' she said sighing, 'I shall have to dree my penance for all my friskings!'

'But, oh, what kindly friskings!' cried Anne, throwing herself into those tender arms.

'Little they will reck of kindness out of rule,' sighed the Prioress. 'If only they will send me back to Greystone, then shall I hear of thee, and thou hadst better take Florimond, poor hound, or the Sisters at York may put him to penance too!'

Henry Clifford was able to walk again, though still lame, when, in the early morning of Ascension Day, he and Anne St. John were married in the hall of Master Lorimer's house by a trusty priest of Barnet, and in the afternoon, when the thanksgiving worship at the church had been gone through, they started in the waggon for the first stage of the journey, to be overtaken at the halting-place by the Prioress and Master Lorimer, who had had to ride into London to finish some business.

And he brought tidings that rendered that wedding-day one of mournful, if peaceful, remembrances.

For he had seen, borne from the Tower, along Cheapside, the bier on which lay the body of King Henry, his hands clasped on his breast, his white face upturned with that heavenly expression which Hal knew so well, enhanced into perfect peace, every toil, every grief at an end.

Whether blood dropped as the procession moved along, Lorimer could not certainly tell. Whether so it was, or whoever shed it, there was no marring the absolute rest and joy that had crowned the 'meek usurper's holy head,' after his dreary half-century of suffering under the retribution of the ancestral sins of two lines of forefathers. All had been undergone in a deep and holy trust and faith such as could render even his hereditary insanity an actual shield from the poignancy of grief.

Tears were shed, not bitter nor vengeful. Such thoughts would have seemed out of place with the memory of the gentle countenance of love, good-will and peace, and as Harry and Anne joined in the service that the Prioress had requested to have in the early daylight before starting, Hal felt that to the hermit saint of his boyhood he verily owed his own self.

CHAPTER XXIII. — BROUGHAM CASTLE

And now am I an Earlis son,
  And not a banished man.
  —NUT-BROWN MAID.

That journey northward in the long summer days was a honeymoon to the young couple. The Prioress left them as much to themselves as possible, trying to rejoice fully in their gladness, and not to think what might have been hers but for that vow of her parents, keeping her hours diligently in preparation for the stricter rule awaiting her.

When they parted she sent Florimond with them, to be restored if she were allowed to return to Greystone, and Anne parted with her with many tears as the truest mother and friend she had ever known.

By this time Harry was able to ride, and the two, with a couple of men-at-arms hired as escort, made their way over the moors, Harry's head throbbing with gladness, as, with a shout of joy, he hailed his own mountain-heads, Helvellyn and Saddleback, in all their purple cloud-like majesty.

They agreed first to go to Dolly's homestead, drawn as much by affection as by prudence. Delight it was to Hal to point out the rocks and bushes of his home; but when he came in sight of Piers and the sheep, the dumb boy broke out into a cry of terror, and rushed away headlong, nor did he turn till he felt Watch's very substantial paws bounding on him in ecstasy.

Watch was indeed a forerunner, for Dolly and her husband could scarcely be induced by his solid presence and caresses to come out and see for themselves that the tall knight and lady were no ghostly shades, nor bewildered travellers, but that this was their own nursling Hal, whom Simon Bunce had reported to be lying dead under a gorse-bush at Barnet, and further that the lovely brunette lady was the little lost child whom Dolly had mothered for a night.

While the happy goodwife was regaling them with the best she had to offer, Hob set forth to announce their arrival at Threlkeld, being not certain what the cautious Sir Lancelot would deem advisable, since the Lancaster race had perished, and York was in the ascendant.

There was a long time to wait, but finally Sir Lancelot himself came riding through the wood, no longer afraid to welcome his stepson at the castle, and the more willing since the bride newly arrived was no maiden of low degree, but a damsel of equal birth and with unquestioned rights.

So all was well, and the lady no longer had to embrace her son in fear and trembling, but to see him a handsome and thoughtful young man, well able to take his place in her halls.

Since he had been actually in arms against King Edward it was not thought safe to assert his claims to his father's domains, but the lady gave up to him a portion of her own inheritance from the Vescis, where he and Anne were able to live in Barden Tower in Yorkshire, not far from Bolton Abbey. So Hal's shepherd days were over, though he still loved country habits and ways. Hob came to be once more his attendant, Dolly was Anne's bower-woman, and Simon Bunce Sir Harry's squire, though he never ceased blaming himself for having left his master, dead as he thought, when even a poor hound was more trusty.

Florimond was restored to the Prioress, who was reinstated at Greystone, a graver woman than before she had set forth, the better for having watched deeper devotion at the Minoresses', and still more for the terrible realities of the battle of Barnet. At Bolton Abbey Harry found monks who encouraged his craving for information on natural science, and could carry him on much farther in these researches than his hermit, though he always maintained that the royal anchorite and prisoner saw farther into heavenly things than any other whom he had known, and that his soul and insight rose the higher with his outward troubles and bodily decay.

So peacefully went the world with them till Henry was one-and-thirty, and then the tidings of Bosworth Field came north. The great tragedy of Plantagenet was complete, and the ambitious and blood-stained house of York, who had avenged the usurpation of Henry of Lancaster, had perished, chiefly by the hands of each other, and the distantly related descendant of John of Gaunt, Henry Tudor, triumphed.

The Threlkelds were not slow to recollect that it was time for the Cliffords to show their heads; moreover, that the St. Johns of Bletso were related to the Tudors. Though now an aged woman, she descended from her hills, called upon her son and his wife with their little nine-year-old son to come with her, and pay homage to the new sovereign in their own names, and rode with them to Westminster.

There a very different monarch from the saint of Harry's memory received and favoured him. The lands of Westmoreland were granted to him as his right, and on their return, Master Lorimer coming by special invitation, the family were welcomed at Brougham Castle, the cradle of their race, where Harry Clifford, no longer an outlaw, began the career thus described:

```
Love had he found in huts where poor men lie,
      His daily teachers had been woods and rills,
   The silence that is in the starry sky,
      The sleep that is among the lonely hills.
```

In him the savage virtue of the race,
  Revenge, and all ferocious thoughts were dead,
Nor did he change, but kept in lofty place
  The wisdom that adversity had bred.

FINIS

www.ingramcontent.com/pod-product-compliance
Lightning Source LLC
Chambersburg PA
CBHW020751020726
47495CB00008B/2376